AF614439

PERFECTLY WRONG

First published in Brazil 2021 by Tulipa Publishing

Original title: Perfeitamente Errada

ISBN 9781069080905

Translation by Laura Machado

Editor	Editorial Coordinator	Proofreader	Cover and Interior
Fernanda Segantini	Mariana Pereira	Caroline Palmier	Laura Machado

---

Mariana Pereira

PERFECTLY WRONG

There are so many people to whom this book could be dedicated, but I could never release it into the world without paying homage to the man who supported it unconditionally: Dr. Ivan Barreira Cheida Faria, also known as, among other things, husband to Angela, Fernanda's father, Miguel and Carolina's grandfather, Thiago's father-in-law, and, most recently the "Ivan constellation".

Covid kept him from being here to encourage me to get in touch with a certain singer, but it was his light and energy that guided us through the entire process of publishing this book.

Perfectly Wrong is for him and for everyone who, to our great sorrow, has now become a part of the starry sky that shines on us at night.

“Yeah, you’re perfectly wrong for me
Hate that you know that I won’t leave
Yeah, you’re perfectly wrong for me”

Perfectly Wrong – Shawn Mendes

PROLOGUE
Elena

I CONSIDERED HIDING BEHIND THE SOFA, WHERE HE wouldn't see me, but that was wishful thinking. Noah would turn the house upside down until he found me. He was furious—no, it was worse than that. He was seething. He wanted revenge and wouldn't stop until he got it.

"Who is he?" my husband yelled, taking heavy steps toward the TV room on the second floor where I was. I had to get out of that house. I needed to find an escape as soon as possible. "WHO'S THE FUCKER YOU'RE SLEEPING WITH?"

"No one!" I repeated senselessly, but he wouldn't listen. "Noah, please, stop! I'm not seeing anyone else!"

It was a ridiculous scene: there I was, pleading for my life to the man who had once promised to love me and make me happy no matter the circumstances. As he marched toward me, the portraits on the side table crashed to the floor. Noah destroyed our happy memories in one fell swoop, and I couldn't let myself think about what he would do to me if he got the chance.

I was cornered between the couch and the wall. Behind me were only windows, and I knew I'd get hurt if I jumped. Noah grabbed the crystal vase we had bought the week before from the side table. It was one of my favorite pieces, and he knew it. According to him, he had been so captivated by the shine in my eyes when I saw it that he simply had to get it.

"Let's see what your lover thinks of your face once it's been cut up by glass shards." A cruel smirk spread across his face, his eyes vacant. "Let's see if he'll still want to fuck you when that perfect skin I've paid for all these years is ruined."

"Noah, please don't do this." I struggled to breathe, scanning my surroundings for a way out.

Honestly, I couldn't care less about my face being ruined. First of all, I didn't have a lover, and second, all I wanted was a divorce! That was all I had said that evening when he got home from work. I had calmly and conciliatorily told him that it wasn't working anymore and that I wanted my old life back. That had been enough to set him off.

"You should've thought of that before cheating on me, Elena! You should've thought about those 'Noah, please don't do this' before sharing his bed like the fucking whore that you are!"

He was so close I could smell him—once a scent I loved, now it sent chills down my spine. He only needed to take a few more steps, and that vase would end up smashed against my face. It scared me less than the anticipated pain from it later. What if shards got in my eyes and left me blind? What would he do if I passed out? Would he keep torturing me until he killed me? What if he thought I'd died and buried me alive? It was then that panic set in. I looked around again and noticed one of the windows was open. Without hesitating, I ran toward it.

"You're not that brave, Elena," he mocked, approaching me with a smirk. "You're afraid of heights, remember? Look down, Elena. Look how far you are from the ground."

Noah was right, and I was terrified of what would happen if I jumped. I was practically counting how many bones might remain intact after jumping from a two-story window, if I even survived it. But nothing terrified me more than the man standing just two feet away. I gazed at his beautiful face, my heart heavy with sorrow as I climbed onto the windowsill, my lungs seemingly rejecting the air I tried to breathe.

"Elena!" His tone changed, a desperate attempt to regain my attention, to manipulate me as he had for nine long years.

My husband reached out, and I closed my eyes, letting myself fall. I felt his nails scrape against my right arm just as my feet lifted off, granting me a strange sense of freedom. Mere moments later, I woke up.

CHAPTER ONE
Elena

I SAT UP IN BED, BREATHLESS, WITH SWEAT TRICKLING down my cheeks. Another night, another nightmare. The day I ran from my now ex-husband haunted me like a curse he'd probably cast before we separated for good. Or should I say, the day I "flew away from my ex-husband"? I rubbed my face, trying to adjust my eyes and figure out where I was. In my bed. The room was dark, indicating it was the middle of the night. My house was completely silent, and I was alone. Thank God!

After everything that had happened the year before, I moved into my own place and started a new life, leaving behind years of submission and insults in an effort to reclaim the Elena I had always been. Unfortunately, what transpired kept reminding me day after day that I was, in some way or another, still trapped. I turned on the lamp on my bedside table. The room was smaller than the one in my old house. Though the judge sentenced Noah to four years in prison and declared everything we had as mine, I hadn't wanted to return to that place to collect my belongings. My parents rushed to Toronto as soon as they heard I'd been in the hospital and took care of everything for me. Shaken as they were, they blamed themselves for a long time for having supported and treated that monster like a son. But how could they have known? How could any of us have predicted such a tragic end to a marriage that once seemed so perfect?

Noah was different. I know what you're going to say—they're always different—but it's the truth. We met in school and became friends almost instantly. As the years went by, we discovered we had more in common than we'd expected. He asked me to prom in high school, and it was then that we shared our first kiss. Noah was the sweetest, kindest, and most polite boy ever, to the point where my parents always took his side whenever we fought. His calm demeanor and soft voice contrasted strikingly with his six-foot height and muscular build. When he wasn't working at a store in town, he spent hours at the gym, lifting more weight than I could count. He was my first everything: boyfriend, man, love.

But after we left Dorchester, a small residential area in Thames Centre, Ontario, and moved to Toronto, things began to change. Noah was accepted into the University of Toronto to study finance, and our families were thrilled! We'd been married for six months, and it was our chance to build a life together in a new city. He was also my biggest supporter when I decided to apply to George Brown College to study marketing, and he was the first person I told when I got in. I can still hear his voice when he said, "I've never been so proud!"

Life was good. At first, we lived in a two-bedroom apartment, supported by our families. We studied full-time, but I managed to work part-time at a coffee shop in our neighborhood, giving us some extra money to spend on our place. Even though our parents covered the rent and bills, it felt empowering to go out with my husband without relying on them for money. It didn't take long for us to buy a beautiful two-story house in a good neighborhood with five bedrooms and plenty of space.

However, after two years in Toronto, Noah's behavior changed completely. He was no longer the happy-go-lucky guy I had met in Dorchester. My husband grew angry about everything, and any minor inconvenience was enough to spark a fight: a towel he didn't like, a dirty glass in the sink, the scent of a lavender candle I had lit. He hurled insults at me for the pettiest reasons, with no filter or consideration. Questions turned into orders, "thank you" vanished from his vocabulary, and "please" was replaced by "now." I thought it was just a phase since Noah had a lot on his plate with finals approaching. He had also started an internship, and I assumed it was just too much at once. I tried my best to stay out of his way and complied with his absurd demands.

I also need to mention that my inability to get pregnant contributed to his anger. We never openly discussed it, but having children was one of our dreams and the biggest expectation our families had for us. No one knew exactly why it hadn't happened, but I wasn't in a hurry. I had just landed a job at Icon Records, an imprint of Universe Music Group, and I was having the time of my life. Before bringing a new life into this world, I wanted to establish a lasting career and secure my place in the industry, to avoid being replaceable. Unfortunately, that was far from what was going through Noah's mind. At one point, he accused me of not getting pregnant because I didn't love him enough. He claimed I was ungrateful and arrogant, that I took our marriage for granted and didn't want to share anything with him because I despised him. In hindsight, I can only thank God for never allowing us to have a child. I don't know what would have happened if I'd had to escape with a baby in my arms.

All these thoughts had been swirling through my mind this past year. I was acutely aware that I'd end up in a mental hospital if they didn't stop. I threw back my covers and made my way to the kitchen, hoping a good cup of English tea I'd bought during my last trip to London would help. Additionally, working for a bit would help clear my mind and allow me to move forward with my life, at least for a day. According to the clock in the kitchen, it was only four-thirty, and I groaned in protest. It was Sunday—I should have been able to sleep for at least another four hours.

On my way back to the bedroom, I paused in the office next to the living room and picked up a file thick with documents. My team and I had been invited to work on SM Project, as I liked to call it, and I needed to study and start the marketing plan. When I say my team and I, I'm referring to the amazing people I worked with directly. With so many specialists around the world, it was easier to collaborate in small teams focused on two or three artists at a time. However, we always kept track of every artist prioritized by the company, working closely with their assistants to ensure everything ran smoothly while their contracts lasted. I didn't like to brag, but I had to admit that wicked good marketing was my specialty, and my team was one of the best in the company. This meant we were invited to work on projects that essentially involved world tours and superstars whose profit could keep the label afloat—like Taryn Stewart. After SM Project, she was next on my list.

When things with Noah started to sour, I contemplated giving up my career numerous times. He would belittle my job, claiming it was ridiculous and that he was embarrassed to say his wife made a living promoting talentless artists. It didn't take long for me to realize it was just another one of his schemes to make me depend on him completely, locking me away from the outside world. Luckily, my parents had taught me that a Vaughan never gives up, so I stayed strong and trusted my decision to continue my path at Icon Records.

I left my mug on the bedside table and settled in among my six pillows. Since I wouldn't be able to go back to sleep and it was far too early for anything else, I figured it'd be a good idea to investigate my next artist a little more. It was always wise to arrive at meetings with my homework done.

SM was basically Sam Martin, the eighteen-year-old singer who had skyrocketed to stardom on a social media platform. He had been with us since 2014, and his albums consistently impressed the finance team, generating more revenue than invested. His first single hit the Top 25 on Billboard right out of the gate, which is one of the best indicators of success, right? For a guy his age, it was pretty impressive.

Of course, opening on a world tour for Taryn Stewart had done wonders for establishing Martin's fame, as she practically dominated the music industry. For Sam, this would only be the fourth time he went on tour, and the third time he'd perform shows around the world. As I had come to expect, the orders were clear: his music career needed to grow big enough that every concert and product he released would be sold out. For that reason, and also because Sam Martin was Canadian and lived in Toronto, Jeremy called me into his office and instructed me to drop everything to focus solely on the SM Project.

The initial plan was for Sam to release his new album soon, with aggressive and incisive marketing. We knew there was no room for error, and Icon Records was investing heavily in this venture, placing more trust than ever in whatever plan we devised for this kid's tour. And since they needed a team to make it all happen, guess who they called for help?

It was past nine when I finally set the papers aside. Five hours of uninterrupted reading had given me excellent ideas for our strategy, and all I needed was a list of songs designated for singles to organize a plan for each. If we executed everything I had in mind, this kid would shoot for the stars in no time.

Taking a deep breath, I smiled to myself, feeling satisfied. I was in such a good mood that I decided to treat myself to breakfast at Tim Horton's, a well-known coffee shop here in Canada. I took my time getting dressed, singing to myself as I walked out of the house toward the nearest shop. I just didn't expect to find it closed.

"You've got to be kidding me," I murmured, vexed. Looking up, I searched for some divine assistance. The sky was a clear and inspiring blue, and the sunshine was lovely, which kept me from turning back. I decided not to let a closed coffee shop ruin my morning and walked a few more blocks to a small, cozy café. Rooster Coffee House wasn't my first choice, mainly because of the distance. It was easier to walk to Tim Horton's, practically around the corner from my house, and I was too lazy to walk unnecessarily. But I had to admit, Rooster was much better. Their muffins tasted like something your grandma would make, and they had the tastiest coffee I'd ever tried.

When I arrived, I ordered a cappuccino and a bagel with cream cheese. Once I found a comfortable armchair by a huge window, I began drafting my marketing plan in the little purple notebook I'd brought for that exact purpose.

I couldn't tell how long I was lost in my thoughts and writing nonstop, but suddenly I began to feel eyes on me. For someone who had been through what I had, it was a terrifying sensation. I glanced away from my notebook, carefully surveying my surroundings. No one was sitting in the armchair next to mine, let alone watching me from outside the shop, yet the feeling of being observed persisted. I took a deep breath, trying not to panic, and continued scanning the café.

That was when I saw him for the first time, sitting on a stool in a distant corner. When our eyes met, he tried and failed miserably to appear nonchalant. A shy smile crept onto his face, and a bright red flush spread from his cheeks to the tips of his ears. It didn't take much effort to recognize him, especially after spending five hours studying everything about him and reviewing the photos in Jeremy's file. I lowered my head and focused on my notebook, which contained nothing but my plans for his career, pondering whether I should introduce myself. I weighed politeness against the many meetings we were already scheduled for and concluded that it would be unnecessary to preemptively introduce ourselves. Truth be told, I just wanted to remain at peace and on my own for a little while longer, which meant I had no interest in socializing anytime soon.

He stood up, and for a split second, I thought he might walk towards me. I prayed he'd walk away, and thankfully, he did. My new project headed to the restroom, giving me a chance to escape. I still had too much to think about and study, with no time to waste on Sam Martin—not then.

CHAPTER TWO
Elena

MONDAY FINALLY ARRIVED, AND I WAS SO EXCITED TO present the SM Project that I woke up an hour early just to prepare. I took a long shower, enjoyed an amazing and fulfilling breakfast, and headed to the office feeling light, chipper, and happy, like a little fairy.

Most of the team hadn't arrived yet, so I invited my faithful sidekicks, Katie and Peter, to hang out at the cafeteria at Icon Records.

"So, how long until we get a little spoiler?" Peter asked, pulling out a chair at the table near the door that we had managed to score. The competition for seating was fierce at that time in the morning.

"Yes, please, Lena! Jeremy took all our projects; it must be something big! I barely slept a wink this weekend; I was so anxious for today's meeting!"

"Calm down, you weirdos," I laughed, stirring my juice nonchalantly. "Let's wait for the rest of the team so I can present the artist and my marketing ideas all at once. What I can tell you now is that it's really cool; the artist is a big deal, and we're going to have a lot of fun."

"Any chance we'll get to travel this time?" Katie asked excitedly.

"Maybe. I'm not sure yet, but I think so."

As they continued to pry for information, my eyes met his again. Sam Martin was standing by the door, looking shocked to see me there. We had a meeting later, but I hadn't expected to run into him in the office this early. Jeremy was to his left, and another suited man was on his right. When our boss spotted us, he decided it was a good idea to stop by our table.

"Good morning, Elena," he said, directing his attention solely at me, a habit that irritated me greatly.

"Jer, good morning." I stood up. "You remember Katie and Peter from my team?"

Once again, he ignored them. "I've got Martin here," he introduced, gesturing to Sam, who looked like he was about to pass out amidst our pleasantries. I could bet he never expected to see the woman he'd tried to seduce in the coffee shop again. And there I was, all smiles and politeness, shaking his hand while trying not to laugh at his expression.

"I thought our meeting was closer to noon. Did I misunderstand?" I asked.

"No, no, it's set for 11 a.m. Sam and his lawyer just came early to settle some contractual and bureaucratic details, but the meeting with the marketing team is still on."

I nodded and took a seat as I watched them look for a table. When I glanced back at my colleagues, I found them staring at me, mouths agape.

"So..." Katie mumbled, her fingers gripping the table so tightly that her knuckles turned white. "Sam Martin is our next project?"

My only response was a wink, followed by the realization that it was time to head upstairs to our floor. The rest of the team was probably already there, and a busy morning awaited us.

"YOU'RE NOT GONNA BELIEVE THIS!" Katie practically burst through the door of the meeting room, startling everyone inside.

"Hey, hold your horses there, girl," I said, trying to hide my laughter. "Good morning, everyone. I scheduled this meeting to announce that we're about to embark on a new project. It's such a significant project that we've been booked to work on everything from the album concept to the world tour production. So get your hearts and minds ready—it's really amazing."

The five pairs of eyes remained fixed on me, waiting for more instructions, but no one dared to speak.

"I'm calling it SM Project to keep it under wraps. SM stands for Sam Martin, the teenage heartthrob and, apparently, Katie's crush. He's our new artist, and our focus will now be entirely on his career."

Katie couldn't stop bouncing in her seat, Morgana was almost hyperventilating, and Jordan looked like he might burst into tears. I had completely forgotten that he had been a Sam Martin fan since the days of his early videos, and he'd been pestering me to catch a glimpse of the singer in the hallways. Maybe I should have talked to him about this sooner, so he'd have had time to prepare his heart. I had no interest in causing any of my employees to have a premature heart attack.

"I understand he's a big deal, but is it really enough to stop working with anyone else?" Matthew asked. "I was enjoying working with that indie group, and our plan for them was solid."

"I know, Matt, but half our team isn't enough for what Icon Records has in store for Martin. We need to elevate his career to intergalactic levels. To do that, the best marketing team in the label—us—will work exclusively with his team, creating the entire aesthetic, visual identity, and marketing plan for both his album and tour. Guys, Icon Records is investing a huge amount of money into this; I can't even say the number. We need to ensure Sam Martin sells enough to justify it and fund the label's holiday party at the end of the year. So, who's ready to take on this challenge with me?"

I wasn't surprised when they exchanged excited glances and every single one of them raised their hands. My team lived and breathed new projects, and nothing excited them more than one as big as this—one capable of frying all our brain cells. They were, after all, my team.

When I said they were awesome, I truly meant it. It didn't take long for all of us to start talking over one another, each contributing ideas better than the last. We took notes on Post-its and arranged them on an impressive timeline. When Victoria and I entered the meeting, we felt confident, sure that everything would go perfectly.

Vicky was one of the most dedicated members of my team. They were all incredible, but I couldn't bring Katie to a meeting like this one, for instance. Fainting would be the best she could manage in front of Martin, effectively ruining all our hard work. Victoria was different. She possessed exceptional communication skills and was a tremendous help in preparing presentations, in addition to being highly organized. No matter how many papers and files we brought, she always had everything ready to present at the right moment.

On the other hand, Martin didn't seem prepared for the meeting. He looked quite uncomfortable around us—or more accurately, around me. I tried my best to avoid his gaze, thinking it might help put him at ease, but it was impossible. Sam had this strange energy that practically compelled me to meet his brown eyes. At one point, we locked eyes, and it was so intense that he became agitated and dropped his glass of water, soaking the entire table. And, man, could he talk! It was as if some supernatural force had taken over, preventing him from stopping!

"So, before we can redefine the points you made, we need to know where you stand with the new album," I said to his team. "Is there an estimated release date? How is it progressing? How many singles will we have to work with?"

Sam and the others exchanged glances. "Actually," he started, "we don't have much ready yet. I have four songs written, and we're about to start recording, but that's it."

"Our star isn't in a great place with his writing," his manager explained, trying to elicit sympathy. "So we're waiting for inspiration to finish the album."

Had I misheard? What on earth did he mean by "our star isn't in a good place"? That they didn't have anything finished or defined? How were we supposed to promote something that didn't even exist?

"I see." I attempted to mask my shock but barely succeeded. It was a lie… I didn't "see" anything. "So, what are we promoting then? A greatest hits tour?"

Jeremy was taken aback by my question, his eyes widening to the point where I expected them to pop out of his sockets and land on the table. The manager took a deep breath, and Sam appeared embarrassed. It wasn't uncommon for struggling artists to release an album of past hits to hold onto their fans for a little longer, but, as I mentioned, those were artists on the decline.

"I think we'll have to redo all our planning and marketing strategy." Victoria sounded frustrated, and I understood her feelings. We had very little time to prepare and had done our best to create a solid plan for Sam Martin. When we were finally ready to set a date, we faced the reality that there wasn't even a flipping album!

"Why would you? It's a fantastic plan; I really like it." Sam nearly jumped out of his seat, despair taking control of his perfectly chiseled jaw.

Vicky took a deep breath, probably counting to ten in her head, clearly trying to avoid ending the meeting by punching the singer in the nose. I appreciated her restraint and thanked her with an encouraging smile. Honestly, at that moment, I would have let her advance over the table and pull his hair just to see if it would spark some inspiration in him. Who knows, right? A little excitement could work wonders, firing up his brain cells and getting whatever was inside him flowing again.

"Because we based our plan on a specific timeline. Your tour dates were carefully chosen based on school holidays and other factors. Your downtime was actually scheduled for the low season of concerts on each continent. Now, since we have no idea when to start, the entire plan needs to change. We need to redo everything!"

And that's how our first meeting with our new prince of pop came to an end. Victoria and I returned to our room to inform the others about all the news we didn't even have.

Man, let me tell you something: you should never underestimate the power of the universe. Seriously! I heard that Sam had other meetings around the office, but I had no idea he would show up at my desk, asking for a private meeting at the end of my workday.

"We can use this room," I suggested, inviting him into our creative area filled with sofas and scattered paper and crayons. This was where our brainstorming sessions happened, where we unleashed our wildest ideas and then organized them into something coherent. It wasn't the most suitable setting for the kind of meeting Martin had in mind, but I wasn't in the mood to hunt for an empty room.

"I know it's not the best time to clear things up or anything," he began. "But I didn't want you to have the wrong impression."

What exactly was he referring to? His awkward attempt to flirt with me at the coffee shop, which had led to an uncomfortable reunion? Or the meeting where we discovered there was no album to promote? I simply nodded, signaling that he had my attention.

"I'm doing my best to write the song so we can finish the album on time." Oh, that. "But I haven't been feeling very inspired. My agent pressuring me has only made it worse."

"Right. Why are you telling me this?"

He shifted on the sofa, clearly uncomfortable. "Because I could tell you guys were frustrated, to say the least, with the outcome of the meeting. I know you had very little time, and your team is only working with me now, so I wanted you to know that I really loved your plan and appreciate all the effort you've put into this."

It was heartening to see him being so honest. All I saw then was a young man doing his best to deserve the opportunity that had been handed to him, even if he didn't quite grasp what that contract really meant. Among so many artists, Icon Records had chosen him, and Martin knew he had to deliver in return. There's no such thing as a free lunch, after all.

"Sam," I said, trying to keep my tone conciliatory. "Things don't always come easily, but you're here for a reason. I know what talent is. We don't sign people who can't at least earn back the money invested in them. Just remember, success and fame are like a train: you're on it, and suddenly someone new takes your seat. If something else is distracting you right now, we need to know. It's better to tell us you need more time so you can eventually bring something solid to the table than to push hard when you're not ready. Is there anything I can do to help you? Not with marketing. We're going to work together for a long time, and I hope we can establish a good working rapport, but what can I do for you as a person?"

And that's how I ended up in an apartment in the Trinity Bellwoods area, near Little Italy, sitting cross-legged on the floor, eating pizza and playing video games with Sam Martin. His team had rented the place on Manning Street to serve as a temporary home for the singer until renovations on his newly purchased apartment were complete. I thought he'd say, "No worries, I've got it handled, everything will be fine," and we'd move on with our lives. Instead, he asked me to dinner, which I politely declined for many reasons. Sam insisted he knew it wasn't a good idea for us to go out together, but no one would see us in his apartment. We could order something and enjoy each other's company for a while. The worst part? That actually sounded good to me.

After beating him three times at Mario Kart, we talked about his new album. Sam wasn't suffering from writer's block; rather, it was his pride that prevented him from letting others help. His songs were well-written, at least as far as my musical knowledge went, and they would easily fit any melody. Even though his team liked them too, they felt something was missing. I knew what it was: his songs lacked commercial appeal. They would be perfect for when he had established himself enough to do anything he wanted, but that wasn't the case now. He needed something catchy, something that would draw new fans to his music.

The label had offered many expensive and experienced partners from the music industry to help, but their styles clashed, and Martin was growing frustrated at not being able to deliver what Icon Records wanted.

"Why don't you try writing new songs?" I suggested. We were still sitting on the living room floor, papers scattered around us as I read through the lyrics of songs he had written but never performed. "I mean, they're amazing, but they're not working the way Icon Records wants, so maybe you should change your approach."

He didn't seem convinced but acknowledged my advice, knowing it was true. Every artist needs to adapt to the label until they're strong enough to succeed and sell without commercial assistance. Beyond that, there was no way to proceed. Music was the most important part of my life, and I loved it. I listened from the moment I woke up until I went to bed, but I couldn't deny it: music is a product, like any other. People invest time and money into writing melodies, recording, and trying to convince others it's good. There was no way for us to release an album we weren't 100 percent sure would sell.

"Look, I've got to get going. Tomorrow is a big day for my team, and we have a lot to do from now on. I promise we're going to create the best marketing plan for you, Sam. We want you to grow in the industry and become one of the biggest artists out there." A genuine smile spread across his face. It was cute. "Think about what I said; open your heart and mind. You can do this."

I gave him a kiss on the cheek, like I would probably do with a nephew. He offered to take me home, but that wasn't necessary. I ordered a cab and stepped out into the cold Toronto night, counting the seconds until I could finally see my bed again.

The following week felt like hell, and when Friday finally arrived, I was ready to set off fireworks. After endless hours of Jeremy trying to teach me how to do my job, all I wanted was to go home, eat something, take a long bath, and hibernate in bed until Monday. My plan was to not even get up for food, which was very unlike me, but I was utterly exhausted and needed the rest. And just so you know, Sam Martin didn't show his face at the office for the rest of the week.

I kicked off my shoes in the foyer and walked barefoot to the kitchen. My stomach had been grumbling for a while, and I figured I should take care of it before my hibernation began. I wouldn't take too long—just a sandwich and some wine would suffice. I lit a candle by the fridge, placing it atop a wooden box where I kept my tea. The scent of lavender quickly filled the room, and I breathed in deeply, allowing the first hints of peace to wash over me.

I opened the fridge and pulled out some ham and catupiry, along with the wine. If you've never heard of catupiry, it's time for a little education. Have you ever tasted cream cheese? That delightful stuff we all know? Well, catupiry is even better! Imagine cream cheese made for humans, while catupiry is made for the divine. When Jesus came to Earth, He likely said, "Son, take this recipe with you and leave it somewhere," and He left it in Brazil. Just so you know, catupiry is lightly processed cheese that complements just about everything. They put it on pizza, hot dogs, and it tastes divine in any dish. Every time I visit the Brazilian market around the corner, I spend a shameful amount on it, but I have no regrets—it's always worth it.

I took a spoonful of catupiry and spread it on the bread I had left sliced on the counter. A few slices of ham later, and it was perfect. The first bite was pure ecstasy! It was so good that I immediately forgot about the stressful week I'd just endured, the team working tirelessly and blindly each day. I didn't waste any time moving to the table; I simply stood there, savoring the wonderful sensation of food settling in my stomach.

About fifteen minutes after I got home, the doorbell rang, interrupting my blissful moment. Who the hell was brave enough to disrupt my peace? A shiver ran down my spine. It couldn't be! Noah wasn't stupid enough to come to my house, knowing full well I'd call the cops. Besides, he was in jail—it wasn't even possible. The doorbell rang again. I took a deep breath, leaving my sandwich on the plate, and approached the front door. Still a bit traumatized, I sneaked a peek through the small glass pane above the door.

"What the heck?" Thank God, Noah wasn't on the other side! Instead, it was... "Sam? What are you doing here?" I asked, opening the door.

"Hey!" He greeted me with a charming smile, adjusting the guitar strap on his shoulder. "I was passing by and thought I'd repay your visit. Plus, I have a new song, and I'd love your input."

I was completely taken aback. What the heck was happening?

"Okay, first of all, you weren't just passing by. You live pretty far from here, and I don't believe in coincidences, especially when you happen to have a new song to show me. Also, I don't babysit in my spare time."

He laughed and tilted his head, unfazed by my rudeness. "Aren't you going to invite me in?"

To my rational side, the right answer was "No, man, go away and leave me alone!" But my parents raised me to be more polite than I wanted to be, so I stepped aside for him to come in. As he walked past me, I inhaled his scent and felt a bit dizzy for a second. Despite being at the peak of his eighteen years, Sam's cologne was different—unique, unlike anything I had encountered before. I shook my head and dismissed the thought before closing the door.

"And by the way," he was saying, "I'm grown, okay? I don't need a babysitter."

"Great," I grunted, heading back to the kitchen. Not even Sam Martin could stand between me and dinner, no matter how good he smelled.

"Sorry, I guess I came at a bad time."

"No worries. Help yourself if you want." I gestured to the ingredients still on the counter.

"Thanks, but I ate on the way."

I nodded, and the kitchen fell into silence. As I finished eating my sandwich, I noticed a curious Sam Martin standing a few meters behind me, looking around and taking in every detail of my house.

"Okay, so... how can I help? You said you have a new song to show me?"

"You've got a nice little house," he said with a shy smile. "Very cozy."

I had no idea how to tell him that yes, it was a nice, cozy place that I could only truly enjoy once he left and let me relish my solitude and my bathtub. Goddamn politeness!

I brought him to the living room and gestured toward the couch. Before making himself comfortable, he respectfully waited for me to sit on the other couch. It was starting to get to me how he could be so good-looking, smell so amazing, and still be a gentleman all at once. He cleared his throat, getting my attention, and I nodded for him to begin.

"Well, the song isn't finished yet. I was hoping you could share some ideas for it."

"I don't know if I can contribute much, Sam," I admitted. "No false modesty here—I'm good at writing, but I've never been involved in songwriting. There are some nuances in that area that I obviously don't master."

"Just listen." He winked as he said it, which was quite attractive, I might add.

His fingers started to pluck the strings, creating a light, almost cheerful melody. I watched his large hands skillfully sliding over the instrument when his voice filled the room.

"I saw you for the first time / in a faraway coffee shop / You just looked at me once / My heart sped up and my hands shook / and that was enough."

Coffee shop? Looked at him once? What the...

"You asked your friends about me / and that was more than I could expect / Because I've been asking about you / not knowing you were already in my head."

To say I was shocked was an understatement for the expression on my face. Sam noticed right away, and to my great despair, he smiled that timid grin of his. He arched his brows ever so slightly, almost imperceptibly, but adorably all the same.

"Thinking of you makes me restless / I get nervous when you look at me / Anxiety takes over / when you stand next to me."

Let's get things into perspective for a moment: I had a very nice guy in front of me—though he was only eighteen—on my couch, singing a song that was essentially about us, and I had absolutely no idea what to do, think, or say. He caught me completely off guard; I never expected this in a million years. And the worst part? He wouldn't shut up. Sam Martin never shut the hell up!

"I talk way too much when I'm near you / I get embarrassed when your eyes are on me / But the thought of never having you makes me panic."

His voice faded with the last notes of his guitar, and for what felt like an eternity, neither of us spoke. He looked at me anxiously, waiting for a reaction—a positive one, at that—to his latest masterpiece. I, on the other hand, stared at him in disbelief. Sam Martin had written a song about an innocent moment we shared, and if that wasn't a sign that things were going awry, I couldn't guess what was.

"So?" He broke the silence first.

I blinked a couple of times, trying to process the situation. "Listen, I want to explain the part where you said I asked my friends about you. That was professionally—"

"No need to explain," he cut me off with a smirk. A tiny dimple appeared on his chin, and my eyes immediately went to it. "I just wanted to say I've been asking about you too. I mean, it's not unrequited, you know?"

If I knew? IF I KNEW? Oh, my boy, you've completely lost it!

"Sam, there's been a mistake!"

"There's no mistake." He set his guitar aside and knelt in front of me. "I know we've only just met, but we can take things slow."

I jumped off the couch, moving away from him. That boy's cologne was intoxicating, practically searing itself into my nostrils. It didn't take long for me to realize I was panting, feeling a bit intimidated by the whole situation. Here I was, a woman ten years older than this boy, feeling like a deer in headlights.

"What the hell are you talking about? Are you insane?" I practically yelled. "Martin, there's no chance in hell of us taking anything slow, even at the slowest pace for humankind."

He looked surprised but also excited. "Really? I thought it'd be better for us, but I'm cool; we can go as fast as you want."

My jaw dropped. That was definitely not what I meant. I could feel my whole face burning as I looked around for a way out.

"I need a drink." I practically ran to the kitchen, with Sam following right behind me. The glass of wine I'd been drinking was still on the counter, abandoned when he interrupted me, and in a fit of despair, I downed it in one go. "There's orange juice in the fridge if you want." I rested my hands on the counter and closed my eyes, taking three deep breaths. My head was spinning, and I wasn't sure if it was because of the wine or the entire situation. When I turned back around, he looked offended. "What? You're not old enough to drink. Not to mention, even when you're sober, you cause way too much trouble."

"All right, I get it already."

"Jesus Christ, finally!" I threw my arms up, thanking divine intervention for bringing some light into his empty skull.

"I know it's too much to take in, so I'm just going to let you think about it," he said, moving even closer to me. My heart raced, and I tried to step back, but my back was already pressed against the counter. "Maybe the song was too much. It wasn't my intention to frighten you; I'm sorry."

His voice was soft as velvet, and his brown eyes searched mine with a mixture of interest and understanding. Sam gently brushed a lock of hair away from my face and tucked it behind my ear, stroking my cheek with his thumb and causing my skin to tingle. I could feel his breath on my lips, and for a split second, I thought he was going to kiss me. I couldn't guarantee that I wouldn't enjoy it, but for God's sake, he was only eighteen.

"I'll see you later." He kissed the corner of my lips, and I almost had a heart attack. Just when I thought that hurricane of a boy had finally left, he poked his head back into the kitchen with a smirk on his face. "Just so you know, Spanish wines are my favorite!"

With a wink, he left.

CHAPTER THREE
Elena

SPANISH WINE! WHO THE HELL DID SAM MARTIN THINK he was, sharing private information like that with someone he barely knew? What was wrong with him, aside from his obvious lack of judgment?

I was wandering through the aisles at Whole Foods, murmuring to myself, when I spotted him on the cover of a magazine. Sam's smile could light up an entire town, and his jawline was ridiculously sharp. I overheard two teenage girls talking about how cute he was and how seductive his voice sounded, and I couldn't help but roll my eyes. Why was everyone so obsessed with him? He was just a pretty face with a thing for Spanish wine.

I ended up in the beverage section, and as I browsed, I noticed the Spanish wines. Even though I preferred Portuguese, I figured it couldn't hurt to check them out. And yes, I threw two bottles of the Spanish ones into my cart. Deal with it.

Just as I was about to finish at the checkout, someone stepped up beside me, and I froze. I tried to get a glimpse out of the corner of my eye, but the guy was so tall I couldn't see his face right away. But when his cologne hit me like a wave, I knew exactly who it was.

"That's a good one," he said, picking up one of the bottles I'd just bought. His voice was so close to my ear that shivers ran down my spine. "Not my favourite, but it'll do."

I closed my eyes briefly. "What are you doing here?"

"Well, I've been waiting for some feedback on my song, which you never gave me." Sam sounded a little frustrated. "So, I decided to come ask in person. Oh, let me help you." He grabbed all the bags from my hands, and we walked out of the store. And let me tell you, we were lucky his fans didn't spot him. I glanced up to offer a quick prayer of thanks, only to notice the dark clouds and feel the first few drops of rain.

"Perfect," I muttered, as we started walking towards my place.

And wouldn't you know it? Apparently, God didn't think that was enough. There I was, standing next to a guy barely out of his teens, waiting for feedback on a song he'd written about us. And I had to admit, it was a good song. But apparently, that wasn't enough, because just as we were halfway to my house, the rain came down hard, soaking us both. We tried to run, but it was pointless. By the time we made it inside, we looked like drowned rats. It was pathetic! I rushed to the kitchen, which was right next to the laundry room, forgetting for a second that I couldn't just strip off my clothes with him standing right there.

When I turned to say something, the words slipped away. His white t-shirt was clinging to his chest, and... well, what a chest!

I couldn't stop staring. His abs looked like they were carved out of stone, and I was pretty sure I'd break my hand if I punched him. The odd thing was, his arms weren't huge—not like Noah's. They were defined but still, well, normal. Water dripped from his hair down his face, and he looked like he was on the verge of laughing. In the end, it was me who started chuckling, though he didn't need to know it was from nerves.

"We need to get out of these clothes," he said, pulling off his t-shirt. "Where do you keep your towels?"

I couldn't find my voice. Sam looked even better with just his black jeans on. A wave of emotions surged through me, and I felt like a fool. I wanted to touch him, to feel his skin against my hands, to kiss every inch of him. At the same time, I felt a sharp pang of guilt. He was so young and seemed so... innocent. Or at least that's what I thought.

"Elena!" I jumped at the sound of my name. "Snap out of it, woman. We need towels. I don't want to catch a cold after all that rain."

He was too close, and his scent—different now, more him—filled the space between us. He smelled like hot summer days at the beach, the happiness of spring, and the warmth of a cozy winter night. He smelled like the good life, like safety and comfort. How could someone smell like... home? The air around us thickened with anticipation. I wasn't sure when it started, but we were both barely breathing now, and with each step he took, the tension grew. Sam was nearly pressed against me. All I could see was his chest and the base of his wet neck. God help me, this was so wrong, but I wanted him. So. Fucking. Much.

And I didn't even like him that much, to be honest. I'd barely known the guy—how could I possibly have feelings for him? This was purely physical, all about seduction. It was having someone pay attention to me after so long. It felt like a small victory, knowing how many younger women would give anything to be in my shoes. I thought about the girls in the store, talking about Sam like he was the last man on Earth. I won. After years of being treated like I didn't matter by Noah, here I was, with a guy—desired by so many—breathing heavily because of me. It was unexpectedly empowering.

Desire filled the kitchen. He wanted it; I could feel the heat radiating from his skin. Sam Martin wanted me as much as I wanted him. I could see it in the way his hands clenched and released, the subtle flex of his biceps. I felt his fingers brush my skin as he slowly lifted my t-shirt.

"What are you doing?" I whispered, still too afraid to meet his gaze. Honestly, I was just as scared of my own reaction.

"Helping you out," he replied softly, his hands steady as they stopped just beneath my breasts. It was bold and outrageous, something I should have stopped. Instead, I lifted my arms, letting him undress me. We were both just waiting for that final push.

"Sam, we can't. We shouldn't."

"What?" His voice was teasing, sensual. "Take off our wet clothes after the rain?"

"You know what I mean." My voice wavered. What was he doing to me?

"You want this, Elena. You want it as much as I do. **Just say the word. You won't regret it."**

I didn't want to just say it—I wanted to scream to the world how much I wanted him! How much I needed Sam Martin right then and there.

Avoiding his eyes, I looked down. Oh my God. My breath hitched. He was more than ready. No question about it.

"It's yours if you want it." He traced his fingers down my arms, sending shivers through me.

And I did want it. Screw ethics and professional boundaries. I looked into his eyes, and within seconds we were kissing ferociously. Our tongues battled for dominance, our hands were everywhere. Sam unhooked my bra and began teasing my nipples. In response, I unbuttoned his jeans and freed him. I stroked him gently, and he groaned in approval.

His lips moved to my neck, leaving kisses and soft bites as he unzipped my pants. In one swift motion, he pushed everything to the floor, including my underwear.

"Turn around and bend over the counter," he instructed.

I didn't hesitate or resist. At that moment, I was his, and I turned as he guided, leaning over the counter with my elbows. With his knee, Sam spread my legs, trailing kisses and soft bites down my back.

"You're so beautiful," he murmured between kisses.

"Sam," I breathed, the sound barely audible.

He let out a low chuckle. "What, Elena? All you have to do is ask."

My body was on fire, every inch of me aching for him, but I was too overwhelmed to speak. His hand slid around my waist and down between my legs, making it impossible to think. Somewhere in the back of my mind, I registered the sound of a condom being opened and felt a surge of relief that at least one of us had remembered to be responsible, since I could barely remember my own name.

"Holy fuck," I moaned. All those guitar lessons were definitely paying off. "For God's sake, Sam!"

"As you wish." Without another word, he filled me completely, and in that moment, I forgot every time I'd called him a kid or thought of him as innocent.

"Fuck," I groaned as he moved slowly inside me. His grip on my hips tightened, and he picked up the pace. It hit me then—Sam Martin inside me was one of the most incredible feelings in the world.

"You're amazing," he repeated, his breath hot against the back of my neck. Every word, every touch was driving me to the brink.

"We shouldn't... We can't," I whispered, a rare moment of clarity breaking through the haze, as my whole body trembled.

"Do you want me to stop?" He did, and I gasped at the sudden pause.

"No, please."

Screw it. He could do whatever he wanted, and he knew it. And though I wished it would last forever, I reached my limit after a few more thrusts, shattering around him with an orgasm so sharp and intense, it felt otherworldly.

"Elena." Sam's voice broke as he whispered my name, holding me close as he followed me over the edge.

After a few moments, he stepped back, leaving me with an unexpected sense of emptiness.

"We need a shower," he murmured softly in my ear.

Still dazed, I turned to face him. Sam looked even better now, with beads of sweat on his forehead mingling with the water still dripping from his hair. I reached up to stroke his perfect face, and we kissed, before heading to the bathroom to take a well-deserved shower.

The night before was a blur. As I walked out of my house, leaving Sam completely passed out, I tried to piece together everything that had happened. After we got home and had sex, we took a shower together. We started talking, but that led to a second round. Later, we made sandwiches and ate them while watching a movie, and I fell asleep on his chest. I woke up in my own bed, unsure how I'd ended up there.

I felt confused, guilty, embarrassed—but I couldn't deny it: I was also happy and very satisfied. Beyond the fact that he was ten years younger, I had to remember that Sam was a client, and I was being paid to be around him. No matter how good it felt, it was wrong to take advantage of that situation.

Before leaving, I made us breakfast. Just something simple, but enough to give him the energy to get out of my house. I also left him a note saying I was heading to work and wished him a good week, hoping he'd get the hint not to come back.

"I have some ideas!" Vicky exclaimed as I walked into the office. "I just need to check with Design, but trust me—it's going to be amazing! Oh, and they want us to incorporate flowers. Don't ask."

"Well, you wouldn't be on my team if your ideas weren't at least amazing, but flowers? How are we supposed to connect Sam Martin with flowers?" I laughed and paused by her desk to hear what she had in mind.

We spent hours discussing the project and the research on his fan base. The idea behind the tour was to show everyone that Sam wasn't just the boy from the video platform. People needed to see that he'd grown up and was more than ready to take on the fame he was achieving—and deserved.

"The whole point is to make it look upscale. Everything from the merch to the stage design to the ticket printing needs to feel premium. Parents need to feel like they're paying for an experience, not just a concert," Peter was explaining when a knock interrupted him.

Lola, my assistant, poked her head into the office. "Mr. Martin is here, Lena. He wants to see you."

What?

"Do we have anything scheduled?" Vicky flipped through her planner in a panic.

"No, it's fine," I said. "He's probably here to share some ideas for the project. Lola, can you take him to the creative room? I'll be there in a minute." My assistant nodded and left, and everyone else looked at me, curious. "I spoke to him last week and asked him to bring any ideas he had for the tour. You know, if he thought of anything specific he wanted included. I'll see what he has to say."

"I can go with you." Matt moved to follow, but I stopped him at the door.

"No need. I'll just take some notes on what he says. Help Peter with the paper samples so we can figure out if it's a good budget choice. And we need to find that key visual piece, Matt—the one that represents the entire tour!"

Before he could respond, I left and closed the door behind me.

My heart was racing, and not in a good way.

"Hey!" Sam stood up as I walked in, a huge smile spreading across his face.

"What are you doing here?" I asked, closing the curtains to block the view from the hallway.

"Well, since you didn't leave me a phone number, I had to come by to tell you that last night was incredible."

Oh, God. Sam was a sweet guy—still a bit like a teenager, but sweet.

"Look, you can't just show up at my office unless we have a scheduled meeting."

He looked puzzled. "Why not? I mean, after last night…"

"Sam, you know that shouldn't have happened. It was a mistake."

"Oh." He sounded genuinely hurt.

"I know. I'm sorry." And I was. It had been a great night, but the circumstances weren't ideal. He didn't say anything else, and the silence between us was awkward. "Can we talk about this later? I'm in the middle of brainstorming with my team, and they're waiting for me. Plus, they're already suspicious about you showing up unexpectedly."

"Can I come to your place later?"

"Okay," I agreed without thinking. Damn it.

"See you at seven then!" he said cheerfully, walking out without looking back.

The doorbell rang at exactly 7 p.m. I blame the British and their descendants for this relentless punctuality. I was still brushing my hair and had planned to blow-dry it before he arrived. I rushed to the door and swung it open. There he was, leaning against the frame, arms crossed over his chest, wearing a black shirt that somehow made him look even hotter.

I stepped aside to let him in. He didn't seem particularly happy, but he wasn't exactly angry either. I, on the other hand, was losing my mind over the whole situation. Honestly, I didn't want to break his heart, but some tough decisions had to be made.

"So," he began, "what's going on?"

"First things first: do you want a drink?" I was definitely going to need alcohol for this conversation. "I've got Spanish wine."

"Oh, so now I'm old enough for wine, am I?" Sam chuckled at my reaction and followed me to the kitchen. I poured two glasses and sat next to him at the island. "You're killing me, Lena."

I was taking a sip when he called me that for the first time. The shock of hearing that nickname from him, though we'd been close before, almost made me spit the wine back into the glass. Being called Lena wasn't usually a big deal, but coming from him, it sent shivers through my entire body. Those four letters, spoken in his smooth voice, were dangerous to my sanity.

"Right, you're right. Let's just get this over with." Saying I was nervous would be an understatement. I was shaking from head to toe. "Sam, we work together. We're in the middle of a project that's going to take months, and we can't get involved. It's not professional, and if Jeremy finds out, he'll pull my team from your release. Not to mention, you're too young for me." I knew that last reason sounded flimsy. Age was just a number, but deep down, it felt wrong to be involved with an eighteen-year-old when I was almost thirty.

"I hope you really believe that, because I know you had a good time," he said before taking a generous sip of his wine. "It felt like we connected."

"It's true, but look around, Sam. We started off on the wrong foot, and there's no clear way forward. I can't see a happy ending for us."

The wine was quickly making its way through my system, calming me down. Sam, however, seemed to be processing my words. "Maybe you're right." He gently tapped my nose with his finger, making me blink. "But that doesn't mean we can't enjoy ourselves."

"What?"

He got up from his stool and stood behind me, his hands expertly massaging my shoulders.

"We can keep this between us. Just you and me, in our own bubble, enjoying the time we have." He knew exactly what he was doing. The massage was a calculated move, trying to get me to agree with his ridiculous proposal. “Once the tour’s over, you’ll move on to a new project, and we’ll go our separate ways.”

I wasn’t sure what he meant by “separate ways,” but his strong hands seemed to cast some sort of spell over me. I leaned back against his chest and closed my eyes. His hands moved from my shoulders to the base of my neck, sending shivers through my entire body.

“Do you know the advantage of being older than you?” I asked.

“No idea.”

“I know all your tricks, Mr. Martin.” I stood up from the stool. “You’re not going to win me over with just one massage.”

He flashed that dazzling smile, all white teeth and the dimple in his chin. Something inside me melted.

“Maybe I should try harder to win you over then.” He stepped closer, his eyes locked on mine. “Yes or no, Lena?”

Many different responses ran through my mind:

1. Get the hell out of my house.

2. You’re insane, and I’m calling the cops to report a threat to my mental health.

3. Why don’t you find a girl your own age to pester?

But instead, I jumped on him, grabbing him by the neck and kissing him hard. What was wrong with me? Why couldn’t I get rid of him?

The next thing I knew, we were tangled up on my couch, moaning and murmuring, our clothes strewn everywhere, our bodies slick with sweat, having one of the best nights of my life.

CHAPTER FOUR
Elena

ONE, TWO, THREE, FOUR, FIVE SHIRTS. THREE SKIRTS and two pairs of pants. A pantsuit and some jewellery. I paused to think. Running clothes! Even though I always packed them and never actually used them—too exhausted to go for a run after long days. But, hey, Tokyo has its charm, and I could use that as an excuse.

I was packing my suitcase when Sam came out of the en suite bathroom, wearing only his black boxers and using a towel to dry his hair. “I still don’t get why I can’t come with you,” he muttered.

“Probably because it’s a work trip, not a vacation.” I started placing each item of clothing carefully inside the suitcase. “Besides, let me remind you—we’re just seeing each other. We’re not a couple, and people can’t know about us.” He sighed. “And that, dear, was your idea.”

“Right.” Sam’s smile was laced with sarcasm. “Brilliant idea.”

“We can end things right now if you’d prefer.”

He moved closer and helped me close the suitcase.

“How long are you going to keep throwing that in my face?” Sam took the suitcase from the bed and set it by the door. Lately, we'd been caught in an endless loop, having the same argument for the past month. Since we started this secret relationship, it had been both wonderful and difficult. It felt amazing having someone to come home to at the end of a long day, especially after being alone for so long. Not to mention, he was young, full of energy, and had this "life's just beginning" aura. He was also intense and curious, eager to learn anything—from cooking to sex.

But his desire for a serious relationship could be exhausting. His emotions often overruled his logic, and he craved a level of commitment I wasn't ready to give.

I sat down on the bed, studying his perfectly sculpted face that looked as if it had been hand-carved. He took three deep breaths before sitting beside me. "I'm sorry," he said. "I know we have an agreement, and I'll learn to operate on your terms."

"They're not my terms, Martin. We both want this, but in different ways. Right now, I can't be in a public relationship with you, for a lot of reasons."

"Your career at Icon Records," he pointed out.

"Yes, but not just mine—yours too. We're building something incredible here, and you have years of success ahead. I'm not going to let a scandal ruin that if I can help it."

He held my hand and started tracing his fingers over mine. I hated feeling like I had to lecture him, like I was old enough to have a son his age.

"And I've told you before, I'm not interested in the social expectations that come with a public relationship," I said. "It's not about disrespecting you; it's about respecting myself and giving myself some space right now."

He studied my face for a moment, and I felt my cheeks flush. Sam smiled and gave me a soft kiss.

"Are you ever going to tell me what happened?" His voice was full of concern.

"I don't know." I felt my chest tighten. I didn't want to scare him with the details of my past with Noah. "It wasn't good, Sam. You don't want to know."

He nodded. I stood up and positioned myself between his legs. Sam wrapped his arms around my waist.

"You suggested keeping this quiet, and I agreed. That's the way it has to be, okay? Just know you're free to end this whenever you want."

"I'm not going anywhere," he said firmly.

"Let's not make any promises." I kissed him slowly. More than his scent, I loved the way he tasted. "Promises are made to be broken, and I don't want to put either of us in that position."

I pulled away, and he groaned. "Where are you going?"

"I need to do some research on a new client. I'll be in the living room."

I left the bedroom, leaving Sam alone with his thoughts, which clearly needed sorting out.

I had been researching this Japanese band since Monday. Jeremy was on my case to get every detail needed to convince their managers that bringing the group to Canada was a smart move. I'd worked with some of them before, and they were adamant about negotiating only with me, which was ridiculous, considering I wasn't in finance or legal. I was flying to Tokyo just to be there and make them comfortable with signing. But I'd have a team of lawyers and financial experts with me who would handle the actual negotiations.

After two hours of studying, I rested my head on the desk and closed my eyes. I was practically learning Japanese without ever taking a class. Then a soft melody drifted through the room, and I looked up. Sam was sitting on the couch, strumming his guitar.

"I ask myself if someday she'll be mine," he sang, his eyes focused on the strings. *"If she'll ever tell anyone about me and her / though I'd fight for her with my life / I don't own her heart."*

Was he just singing, or was that a hint?

"How many times will I have to ask? / How many more times will she turn away? I just wish she'd tell me."

That was definitely a hint. But Sam Martin better be ready because Elena Vaughan doesn't play games.

"I don't want to set a fire that'll burn us / but I don't know what else to do / if only she trusted me a little more / She'd know that my heart..."

"Will always be hers," I sang, meeting his gaze.

"For evermore," he continued, smiling. *"I know exactly how you feel / I believe you when you say you care / but did he say anything about love? / I can't lose you to something that isn't real."*

He nodded, encouraging me to go on.

"How many times will I have to ask? / How many more times will she turn away? I just wish she'd tell me."

"I don't want to set a fire that'll burn us / but I don't know what else to do."

"If only she trusted me a little more / she'd know that my heart..."

"Will always be hers." Sam stopped playing, a broad smile spreading across his face.

"No, don't stop," I said. "I love that song."

He shrugged and started playing again. *"If you think you've had enough, then it's done / Though I know it'll never end / Our love is a delicate, sturdy rose / I don't want to set a fire that'll burn us / but I don't know what else to do / if only she trusted me a little more / she'd know that my heart / will always be hers / for evermore."*

Rose. A rose! I jumped up from my chair and ran to my room in search of my phone. I dialled Matt's number, and he answered on the second ring.

"Hi, Lena. How are you?"

"A rose, Matt! That's what we've been looking for!"

"What?" I could hear his excitement, but he was cautious. "And why?"

"He was just singing a song, and it clicked."

"He? Where are you?"

Crap.

"I mean, I was listening to one of his songs on Spotify, looking for inspiration. Then I heard this one, called *Our Love is a Rose.*" Nice save, Elena. "The creative team is insistent on working with flowers. Let's tell them we want roses, or at least have them featured somewhere. We can use it to symbolize the transition from the old Sam Martin to the new, evolved version."

"That actually makes sense." He sounded thoughtful. "Picture a massive rose in the middle of the crowd, like a chandelier, hanging above the audience."

My breath caught as I envisioned it. "Yes, exactly! Matt, I'm flying to Japan tomorrow, so you need to lock this down. Get the design team working with roses everywhere."

"You've got it, boss!"

"And I'm sorry for calling so late!"

"Oh, please, Lena. Good ideas can't wait." He laughed. "But I need to go. Jenna's calling. Have a safe trip tomorrow!"

"Thanks. Say hi to Jen for me."

We hung up, but I was still buzzing with energy. I raced back to the living room and leapt onto the couch, landing on top of Sam.

"Holy—" He was startled and nearly dropped his guitar, notebook, and pen.

"Thank you, thank you, thank you for singing that song!" I said, kissing every inch of his face.

"You're welcome, I guess." He laughed, trying to wiggle away from me. "I didn't expect you to join in."

I sat on his lap and started playing with his hair. "Are you kidding? I did a lot of research before our first meeting. I never show up unprepared, which means I know a lot of your songs."

"Good to know." Sam kissed me just below my ear, smiling. "And what are you planning to do with the rose? Album cover, maybe?"

I rolled my eyes. "You'll have to wait and see. If you thought me singing was a surprise, you have no idea what I'm capable of once I put my team to work." I winked and stood up. "But right now, I just want to get into bed, have great sex, and then sleep."

I held out my hand, and he took it without hesitation. I pulled him up from the couch, and our lips met in a slow, sensual kiss. He wrapped his arms around me so tightly that my feet left the ground.

"Where are we headed?" he asked between kisses. "Bedroom? Kitchen? Your desk? The floor?"

"Are you planning to christen the whole house?"

"Absolutely." He laughed. "And once we're done here, we'll move on to mine. Then my car, your office, every hotel room in Toronto."

"What about airplanes?" I suggested, smiling at the thought. It had always been a fantasy of mine. "In the restroom during turbulence. That would be something."

Sam paused, his eyes gleaming with intrigue. He set me back down and started unbuttoning my shirt. "Sounds like we have some very interesting ideas in the air, eh?"

I smirked and took his hands in mine. "The ideas aren't the only things I want to get interesting, Mr. Martin. Let's go to my room—I want you on my bed."

He followed me eagerly, like the good boy he was. Once we were there, Sam moved towards me, full of desire and determination, but I stepped back before he could touch me. "Take your clothes off," I said.

The atmosphere shifted, and I saw his breathing deepen. Despite his confident exterior, Sam was still an eighteen-year-old, excited but a little nervous. It was time to teach him a few things. He pulled off his shirt and hesitated, looking a bit uncertain.

"What?" I asked, my tone firm. "I'm not helping. Keep going. Pants and underwear."

He unbuttoned his jeans and took everything off in one swift motion, standing completely naked in the middle of my room. And what a sight he was. I approached him, running my hands down his arms. He tried to touch me, but I didn't let him. This was my moment, and I wanted every second of it.

I circled him slowly, trailing my fingers along his abdomen and back. "What are you doing?" he whispered, his eyes half-closed, lips slightly parted.

"Enjoying the view," I replied in a low, sultry voice. "And deciding where to start."

The anticipation was driving me wild, but it was nothing compared to what it was doing to Sam. The thrill of being at my mercy turned him on, and he was more than ready. I moved behind him and started stroking him gently.

"Fuck," he breathed out. "That's torture, Elena!"

"Is it?" I teased, stepping in front of him again, locking eyes. "Let's see what you think of the challenge I have for you."

His eyes sparkled, and he grinned.

"I'm going to please you with my mouth, but you can't come. If you do, no sex until I'm back from Japan. If you can hold back, I'm yours—any way you want me."

"Why are you doing this?" His voice was a mix of shock and excitement. He was loving this.

"So you'll remember me while I'm gone." I bit my lip provocatively and exhaled. "Or we can just have regular sex, but I think you're up for the challenge. What's it going to be?"

"Can I make a counter-offer?"

I rolled my eyes. "Spit it out before I lose interest and entertain myself."

He grinned, probably amused by the thought of me taking matters into my own hands.

"I'll take your challenge, Miss Vaughan." His voice was low and sexy. He'd never called me by my surname before, and it sent shivers through me. "But first, you need to take your clothes off. I don't want to waste time on that later."

That was fair. I agreed. Especially since, with what I had in mind, I'd be begging for him to finish long before I wanted to stop. Being naked would save time.

I stepped back and began taking off my clothes slowly. He tried to touch himself, but as I'd already made clear: this was my moment. "No," I scolded. "It's mine!"

Sam exhaled, more in satisfaction than surprise. When I was down to just my underwear, I knelt in front of him. If you'd asked me what was going through my mind, I wouldn't have been able to explain. Maybe I was just tired of always following orders, tired of people trying to control my life. Do this, read that, write those reports, choose where I'll let you take control next. Screw that. I needed to reclaim some power, and lucky for Sam—or maybe not—my moment of taking it back just happened to be when he was around. And naked.

"You're still wearing clothes," he muttered, shutting his eyes as I wrapped my lips around him.

I wondered if there was any part of this boy's body that wasn't perfect. I teased him with my hands, keeping him in my mouth the entire time, caressing him with my lips, making circular motions with my tongue along his length. Sam was clearly doing his best not to give in, not to lose the challenge—which would mean no second round. But this wasn't the time to be merciful, so I took him deep, all the way to my throat.

"Fuck, Elena," he groaned, and I couldn't help but grin. He gripped my head, trying to steady himself, but my hands were quicker and held him in place. "Shit."

"No," I warned. It would be really frustrating if he couldn't control himself and I had to stick to my promise of no more. But I knew Martin could handle it. For God's sake, he was young, full of hormones, and in perfect health. It's not like he had to worry about coming quickly because of a bad back.

I took him deep again, and when I felt him twitch, I stopped. Oh, no, honey. Don't even think about it. Our eyes locked, and I licked my lips. Sam looked both amazed and desperate. Before I could make another move, he pulled me up and tossed me onto the bed. I squealed in delight.

He was furious, just as I'd hoped. He loomed over me, holding himself up on his arms. We stared at each other for a moment. "This is going to be quick," he warned. "You've driven me crazy. I need a good fuck."

I giggled. "I wouldn't expect anything less from you right now." I bit his lower lip, tugging gently. He smiled. "There are condoms in the top drawer of the bedside table."

His eyebrows rose. "Prepared, huh?" He grabbed one and put it on hurriedly.

"Always," I said proudly. "You never know when an eighteen-year-old boy full of energy will show up for—what was it you said? A good fuck?"

"You must get a lot of visits if you bought a whole box," he teased, trying not to laugh.

"Or maybe I was just waiting for a particular boy to shut up." I winked.

Sam kissed me hard and started tracing his fingers over my underwear. "How attached are you to these?" His fingers played with the lace waistband. Considering it was a beautiful black set from Victoria's Secret, I liked it a lot. But I liked what he could do with it even more.

"Buy me two more of these later, and you can do whatever you want."

"Deal," he said, and my underwear became two pieces of fabric in his hands. The sound of ripping lace in a moment like this is surprisingly sexy.

He lifted my legs, positioning his arms behind my knees. As promised, it was quick and intense. I shuddered, first in surprise and then in pure pleasure. The sensation of having him inside me was incredible. He kissed me deeply and began thrusting hard. Our bodies collided with every movement, and my breath came in rapid bursts.

"This is..." I tried to speak, but I couldn't. My entire body was on edge, and the electricity between us was overwhelming. We were good together. No, we were amazing together.

"I know," he whispered against my neck. His moans grew louder, his skin glistening with sweat.

I felt my muscles tightening and clung to the back of his neck, digging my nails into his skin.

"Come on, Lena," he urged in my ear. "Come for me."

Not that he needed to ask—I was already there—but his low, deep voice was the final push, and I climaxed around him, pulling Sam over the edge with me in a powerful release that made him groan my name.

He collapsed on top of me, still inside, our bodies entangled. I could feel his breath slowing, his heart rate returning to normal. We lay there in silence, and I ran my fingers through his hair.

"A kiss for your thoughts," he said, his voice tired.

"Just a kiss?" I teased. "I think you can offer more than that, Mr. Martin."

He laughed softly.

"I'm just thinking about tomorrow's trip. It's going to be exhausting with all the negotiations I'm not interested in."

"Then why are you going?" he asked, lifting his head to look at me.

“Because I follow orders,” I grumbled. “What about you? What are you thinking?”

His cheeks flushed. “About a song I’ve been working on.” His shy smile appeared, and it was the cutest thing ever.

“Oh, so we’re making progress?”

The rest of his face turned red too.

“I think so. I have some new songs I’m planning to show the producers soon. Just need to finish one I started earlier today.”

“Can I see the lyrics? Or maybe you can play them for me?”

He shook his head. “Not yet. They’re still rough. I need a more professional opinion first.”

I rolled my eyes, and Sam chuckled. I wasn’t going to push him. If he wasn’t ready to share, that was fine. I was just happy he was writing again and that we’d have something to work with soon.

It was our fourth meeting in three days. The band’s team’s demands were starting to get on my nerves. I understood they deserved to be heard, given their popularity, but this was getting out of hand. Did they think we were amateurs who couldn’t handle a group of up-and-coming singers? We’ve been doing this for decades.

My phone buzzed in the middle of the meeting, and I glanced at it.

Call me as soon as you can! SM

Before I left, Sam had asked for my number. I tried to avoid giving it to him, but the guy was persistent. In my opinion, what we had wasn’t serious enough to be sharing personal information like phone numbers or email addresses. I was already sharing my bed—what more did he want?

One of our lawyers shot me a look. Another request for changes to the contract had just come in, and the Japanese representatives were waiting for my response. I wanted to tell them all to go to hell and walk out of that room, especially now that they were demanding their own marketing specialist work with our team, essentially replacing my colleagues. That really rubbed me the wrong way.

"Gentlemen, I have to say I'm a bit offended by your request," I said, keeping my tone professional. "With all due respect, your marketing team isn't familiar with our target audience. How could they create a marketing plan based on what they know of the Japanese market in Canada? I understand your concerns, and we will keep you informed of all our projects. That's the best I can promise from our marketing team."

Murmurs went around the table. From our side, there was unanimous approval. Who did they think they were, trying to dictate how we did our job? We were already offering far more than the band was truly worth. On their side, there were raised voices, but I didn't care.

"You know, she's right," Rento, their marketing manager, finally said. "We could take the lead on this, but it would take us months to research the Canadian audience. Elena's team already knows them well, which will save us a lot of time. And she'll be kind enough to share everything with us. We've worked together before, and you can trust in her team's excellence and professionalism."

That was unexpected. I almost thanked Rento, but I just nodded, hoping everyone else would agree. And they did.

We wrapped up the meeting, and I stepped out of the room, immediately pulling out my phone to call the number that had texted me.

"Hey, how are you?" Sam answered almost instantly, his voice bright with excitement. "How are the negotiations going?"

"They're driving me crazy," I replied, still annoyed, as I ducked into the nearest restroom for some privacy.

"I'm sorry to hear that. But I have some news, and I hope it'll cheer you up."

"Really? Let's hear it, Martin. You went to the studio, recorded an entire album, and now we can finally get to work, right?"

I must have sounded too eager because Sam laughed nervously. "Not quite, but we're getting there, I promise. Before I tell you the big news, I have a question for you. Do you got plans tonight?"

That was an odd question coming from someone who was many time zones away.

"Yes. I'm going to put on my pyjamas and sleep like a baby, hoping not to dream about managers and Japanese bands. Why?"

"I was thinking of, I don't know, flying to Japan to spend the rest of the week with you."

I laughed. "Sure, right." But he didn't say anything. "Wait, are you serious?"

"Yes!" Sam sounded anxious. "I'm about to get on the plane."

I sat down on the toilet lid in shock. "You can't come! You're famous here; people will start questioning why you're in Japan! What am I supposed to tell Icon Records? That I've taken up a side gig as a tour guide in Tokyo?"

He sighed. "We'll figure it out once I'm there. Just text me your hotel and room number so I can find you. And Lena?"

"What?" I felt a headache coming on.

"Try not to fall asleep. It's just a few hours, and I have a surprise for you."

Then he hung up. I left the restroom feeling a mix of tension, shock, and confusion. But after a moment of thinking, I realized he had to be joking. There was no way Sam would fly seventeen hours just to see me. Even though I was more than worth the trip, he had to be bluffing, and I had nothing to worry about. Deciding to play along, I texted him:

Keito Plaza Hotel, room 321! Xx

Two can play this game, darling!

"Elena," I heard Rento call out. "Ready for lunch?"

"Absolutely, let's go."

Feeling light as a feather, knowing I wouldn't have to deal with an unexpected visitor that evening, I headed out to lunch with my colleagues. All that stress had left me starving, and I was more than ready for some Japanese food.

And I'd been right. Sam didn't show up that evening, but it was odd that he didn't text or say anything else either. Even though I'd mentioned my number was for emergencies or if he needed help, he'd texted me a few times while we were apart. I replied once or twice and ignored the rest.

After a well-deserved bath, I put on my dark blue pyjamas covered in polar bear prints. Exhausted, I refused to leave my room to eat. Just as I finished drying my hair, a knock at the door indicated room service had arrived.

I tried to stay awake, watching something on Netflix, but my eyes were heavy, and I could barely keep them open. Hugging the extra pillow, I fell asleep within seconds, only to be woken up hours later by the sound of my phone buzzing.

"Hmm?" I mumbled groggily.

"Hey." Sam's voice came through the speaker. "Can you open the door?"

"Martin, go to bed. There's no way you're in Japan, standing outside my room."

I heard a single knock.

"Did you hear that?"

I sat up in bed. Another knock.

"And that?"

"You didn't…"

He laughed.

"Of course, I did. Now, please open the door?"

I hung up and stumbled to the entrance, opening the door just a crack to peek out.

"What the hell?" I opened it all the way, and a grinning Sam Martin walked in without waiting for permission. As he passed me, his arm wrapped around my waist, and he pulled me into a deep, lingering kiss, clearly having missed me. It was intense—more than I could handle in my sleepy state.

"Did you miss me?" Sam asked in the sweetest voice.

"No," I almost shouted. "And I'm definitely not going to miss you after I kill you! What are you doing here?"

I locked the door and caught a glimpse of myself in the mirror. His kiss had left my lips red, and my hair was a mess. It was five in the morning, and I couldn't believe he'd woken me up at this hour.

"I told you I was coming. You should believe me more often. And by the way, I missed you." He shrugged and placed his suitcase next to mine.

I blinked a few times. This had to be a dream. A nightmare, more accurately.

"Okay," I said, marching back to the bed. "I'm going back to sleep, and when I wake up, I'll be alone in my room, and you'll be back in Canada, and everything will be fine."

"I wouldn't do that if I were you," he teased, and I stopped, glaring at him.

"And why not?"

A wicked grin spread across his face. "Doctors say morning sex is the best way to start the day."

Though he tried to keep a straight face, his eyes sparkled with mischief.

I was furious. Completely pissed off. But I couldn't deny that Sam was like a breath of fresh air, pulling me back to a time I'd barely had the chance to enjoy—the carefree days of being twenty. Back then, I'd already been dating Noah. He was my first and only, so I never got the chance to go a little wild. Honestly, I wanted to experience that. To jump on Sam and make love until morning.

It didn't matter how much joy Sam brought into my life, though—I didn't want him to get hurt. And that was inevitable. He couldn't see the reality of our casual relationship, not clearly. The fact that he'd spent an absurd amount of money on a last-minute flight, travelling seventeen hours from Toronto to Tokyo just to see me, was alarming.

"Do you love me, Sam?" The question slipped out before I could stop it. He took a step back.

"Love?" He seemed to be processing the word, rubbing the back of his neck. "I'm not sure. What's the difference between loving someone and adoring them? Which one leads you down the aisle, gets you two kids and a dog?"

I took a deep breath, almost panicking. "Love, I think."

"Then I adore you," he said, his grin widening.

"Great." I could feel my heart racing. "Perfect."

There was still time to save his soul, it seemed.

Sam stepped closer, brushing his hand against my cheek. He began kissing my face, his lips igniting a fire everywhere they touched, while his hand moved to my neck. I closed my eyes and let myself enjoy the sensation. His hands were skilled, probably from endless hours playing the guitar. When his lips reached the base of my ear, I pulled back, pushing him away.

"What?" He looked confused.

"You're not going to win me over with sex, Martin," I said, my tone stern.

"Oh, that's a shame." He kicked off his shoes and began undressing. "Especially after you see the gift I brought you. I think you'll regret it."

Sam sprawled across my bed, now wearing only his trademark

black boxers, looking more irresistible than ever. I could easily ride him for hours and not feel guilty about it.

"Where is it?" I asked, intrigued. He pointed to his suitcase and told me to grab a pink package from inside. "Victoria's Secret?"

Oh. My underwear!

When I opened it, I was stunned. He'd promised me two, but there were dozens in the bag—all different styles, colours, and fabrics. Some were pretty daring, too.

"Twenty-two pairs, in case you're wondering." He beamed with pride. "Two because I promised, and the other twenty so I can rip more without you getting mad at me."

I couldn't hold back my laughter. I spread them out beside him on the bed and asked Sam to pick one.

"Ha-ha," he mocked, "I see the regret is kicking in sooner than expected."

He chose a black set, similar to the one he'd torn apart before. The difference was this one was a thong.

I went to the bathroom to change and start the day as he'd suggested. I was already awake—might as well make the most of it, right?

Right.

CHAPTER FIVE

Elena

THAT THURSDAY HAD STARTED WAY TOO EARLY—BUT in the best way. After what Sam had called, "the best morning sex of my life, we definitely need to do this again," I was getting ready for work while he took a shower.

"She never hides the truth, and I think that's amazing / It's hard to find someone like this," he sang at the top of his lungs, as if performing on stage. *"She's hardly a Greek goddess / but I love her with all of me."*

I rolled my eyes and smiled. His voice was beautiful, and he wasn't even trying to stay on pitch.

"Even if I tried, this won't end here / Even though she's won this time / she says I'm not good enough."

"But I can't stay away," I sang softly, keeping up with his loud performance. I peeked into the bathroom, and he winked at me. "If you keep this up, we're going to get kicked out of the hotel. How am I supposed to explain that to the press? Can you imagine the headlines? *Sam Martin kicked out of hotel for singing in the shower.*"

He burst into laughter. “Are you saying I’m not a good singer, Miss Vaughan?” He raised his eyebrows playfully.

“You just sang that I’m not a Greek goddess. Be grateful I’m being nice when I tell you to tone it down.”

“I didn’t say that.” He couldn’t stop laughing. “I was just singing my song.”

“Oh, I see,” I teased. “You sing that after having sex with me? Very classy. I’m flattered.”

“At least I said you’re honest and never hide the truth.” Sam shrugged, a mischievous smile on his face.

“You’re ridiculous.”

I let him finish his shower and went back to the room to get dressed. As I was putting on my shoes, Sam came up behind me, wrapping his arms around my waist and making me jump.

“Greek goddess is the least of what you are,” he whispered, kissing the spot just behind my ear. He turned me around and looked into my eyes. “You’re my summer day in the middle of winter.”

I cupped his face and kissed him lightly. We stood there, gazing at each other for a few seconds, lost in our thoughts. Then my phone buzzed, reminding me the van was waiting for our team.

“You’re a lucky bastard to have me in your life!” I kissed him again and left, his laughter echoing in the room and bringing a smile to my face all the way to the elevator.

We were almost closing the deal with the Japanese team. The band had been present at the last meeting, and I got to learn more about their daily schedule. It was insane! The boys were kept on a tight leash by their management, and I started to consider doing the same with our artists. Compared to how this band was treated, we were practically mothering ours.

We spent a lot of time talking. I explained how we operated in Canada and shared my thoughts on how best to promote them. It was just a rough idea since I wouldn't be the one guiding them directly. They said their biggest dream was to become as popular as BTS, and they were really grateful for the opportunity from Icon Records. That told me the issue was clearly with their management, who seemed intent on squeezing every penny they could out of the boys.

A text popped up on my phone, and I excused myself to go to the restroom so I could read it without being rude.

What are your plans for lunch today?

I giggled.

I'll have lunch somewhere. You'll have lunch exactly where I expect you to be: in my hotel room. People can't see you, remember?

Sam was like a puppy—constantly needing to be kept in check. If you let him off the leash, he'd get himself into trouble. Unbelievable!

If I order food, people will know I'm here anyway! :(Come on, Lena, let's meet somewhere. I can wear a hat and sunglasses. Please?

As if a hat and sunglasses were enough to hide that perfect jawline of his.

No. Period. I have to get back to work. See you later.

I turned off my phone and went back to the meeting. To my surprise, the band was signing their contract with Icon Records. There were five bottles of champagne and some very happy lawyers.

"I can't believe we finally did it!" one of them exclaimed as I approached the group.

"It feels like heaven!" another murmured. "Thanks for all your help, Elena!"

"Just sign the damn thing so we can get out of here," I joked, and we all laughed. "But first, I want a whole bottle of champagne to myself. I plan on getting drunk to celebrate the end of this torture."

At lunch, we joined the Japanese team at a fancy restaurant just a couple of blocks from the office, conveniently close to the hotel too. I wouldn't have to go back to work afterward, so it was perfect. And remember what I said about champagne? Well, Elena Vaughan had her own bottle and some ideas in mind. All I needed to do was get back to the hotel and meet a certain Canadian boy.

Lunch was going smoothly, although Rento had seated himself on my right and was asking a ton of questions that weren't exactly appropriate for a work setting. I was trying to brush him off politely, but he was testing my patience.

And, of course, when things could go wrong, everything had to go wrong at once. The door to my left opened, and in walked an almost six-foot-five Sam Martin. At that exact moment, Rento decided to grab my hand and bring it to his chest. It was like a scene out of a slow-motion movie. On one side, Sam looked surprised to see me and clearly unsettled by the situation. On the other, I almost fainted when I realized he was outside the hotel and I wanted to punch Rento for the audacity of touching me without my consent. But things got even worse when Marco, one of Icon Records' lawyers, recognized him.

"Sam!" he called out from across the table. "Hey, man, come over here! What are you doing in Japan? Did you know he was here, Elena?"

They greeted each other with a hug, and both sets of eyes turned to me. It was only when Marco said my name and gave me a confused look that I realized Rento was still holding my hand. I yanked it away and forced a smile.

"I didn't," I replied through gritted teeth. Sam gave me a quick hug, but it was long enough for me to whisper in his ear, "Any specific way you'd prefer to die?"

"So?" Marco persisted, clearly not letting this go anytime soon.

"Oh." I could almost hear the gears turning in Sam's head. "You know how it is; I'm looking for inspiration for my new album. I've wanted to visit Japan for a while, and this seemed like the perfect opportunity. I just stopped by to pick up my lunch order."

"That's great." Marco grinned. "Sometimes we need to step out of our comfort zone to create. Right, Elena?"

"Absolutely." I was trembling with anger—furious at the sleazy guy who thought he had a shot with me, and equally frustrated with Sam for risking getting caught. I just wanted to strangle one of them, maybe both. "And you know what I think, Marco? This is a good sign. When our artists step outside their bubble, it always translates into incredible music. I'm sure Martin will deliver some masterpieces. So, how about we let him get back to his creative immersion?"

"And that's why we love this girl and will never let her leave our team." Marco smiled at me warmly. We'd always had a good relationship, and he'd often praised my work, regardless of the situation. He was much older and had a kind of fatherly affection for me. It was sweet and a little awkward at the same time. But he was a good guy. "Enjoy your time in Japan, Sam! See you back in Canada!"

We said our goodbyes, and I returned to my seat at the table.

"Is that your boyfriend?" Rento asked as soon as I sat down.

"Who, Sam?" He nodded. "Of course not! He's a client of Icon Records and just a friend."

"You hugged him." Was the marketing specialist for the Japanese band... jealous? "You've never hugged me."

"And I'm not going to," I snapped. It was harsh, but he didn't seem to get it. When his hand moved closer to my leg, I tipped my champagne glass just right, causing the pink liquid to spill straight into his lap. "Oh my God, Rento! I'm so sorry. Jesus, I'm so clumsy! I'm really sorry!"

After the chaotic scene of cleaning up the mess, the Japanese team decided it was time to get back to work. Well, for them. I was on my way back to the hotel, ready to commit a murder.

From the moment I left the restaurant until I reached the Keio Plaza, I managed to calm down a bit. Maybe I wouldn't kill Sam after all, but he was definitely going to get a lecture.

I saw him as soon as I opened the door. He was sitting on the bed, legs crossed, wearing oversized headphones. The grin on his face told me he had something to share. "Can you hold off on murdering me for a minute?" Sam asked, looking anxious. "I've got something to show you."

I tossed my bag onto our suitcases and sat down across from him. "What is it?"

He handed me the headphones, and I noticed they were plugged into his phone.

"The days you were here before I arrived, I went to the studio with the band. We recorded a song I wrote a while back, and the producer just sent it over. I know you're on the marketing side, but since you know my music, I wanted you to hear it and tell me what you think."

Hmm, that actually was good news. I smiled and squeezed his knee. I put on the headphones, adjusting them over my ears, and Sam hit play.

His voice sounded different—stronger, more self-assured. The melody was powerful, and the lyrics were raw and heartbreaking. He sang about anxiety, depression, and feeling overwhelmed to the point of wanting to give up. I looked over at him; he was biting his lower lip, clearly struggling to keep his, no surprise, anxiety in check.

In the song, he asked for help, spoke about feeling suffocated, and how people didn't understand. They thought all he needed was a drink or a girl, as if his struggles were easy to solve. I found myself getting lost in the melody, remembering my own battles over the years. He was right—no medication could erase memories. I still had nightmares, and there were things I hadn't moved past. It was almost too much, and I wanted to ask him to stop the song.

The high notes filled the headphones, and I closed my eyes. The song was so intense, full of emotion and truth, that I wondered if it was based on his real experiences. Had he really gone through all of that?

But he was also right in the song—it wasn't his style to give up, no matter how overwhelming things felt. That's why he asked for help.

When the final notes played, I felt drained. The song was so heavy, it seemed to sap my energy. I had tears in my eyes, and Sam looked worried. "Are you okay?" he asked.

I took off the headphones and handed them back to him. "Sam, this song is... deep." I struggled to find the right word. "It's beautiful, and it's real. Did you really feel what you sang?"

Now I was the one who was worried. He had started his career so young, and the media could mess with anyone's head.

"Sometimes, yeah." He sighed. "Did you really like it?"

"Of course!" I was confused by his uncertainty. "I mean, I loved it and hated it at the same time. It's an incredible song, but it deals with a really delicate subject. It could help a lot of people. Do you realize that?"

He looked unsure. "I don't know. I've listened to it a few times, and while the melody is good, I can't tell if I did a good job. Maybe we should just scrap it."

"What?" For the first time, I saw him as more than the playful kid or the amazing lover. He was vulnerable, his insecurities filling the room. I knelt in front of him, cupping his face in my hands, forcing him to look at me. "If there's something you're not happy with, that's fine.

We can change it. But it's a beautiful song, with incredible lyrics, and I'm not going to let you dismiss it."

Sam gave me a shy smile, and I kissed him. For the first time, I wanted to shield him from the world.

"Can I listen to it again?" I asked, our lips still close. Sam handed me the headphones, and I settled into his lap. He wrapped his arms around me, and with my head resting on his chest, I closed my eyes and let the music take over.

It felt so good to be with him, even though I knew it was dangerous, considering what I had in mind for my future. Looking back, I couldn't even remember why I kept pushing Sam away. I'd been angry, shocked, and had scolded him more than once, but I always ended up in his arms. The question was: why?

I didn't love him; I knew that much. Maybe if our fling continued for too long, I could develop some sort of feelings. But for now, he was just someone I enjoyed spending time with. And, let's be honest, the sex was amazing. It was funny, really—we barely knew each other. We hadn't had any deep conversations. We spent time together, had sex a few times, and that was it. No profound talks that could change our lives. The song ended for the third time, and I took off the headphones.

"I don't want to get ahead of myself, but we might have a single on our hands." I smiled and kissed him softly. "Good boy!"

"Are you sure?"

"Yes." I stood up and reached for my bag. "And I think we should celebrate!" I pulled out a bottle of champagne, grinning at Sam's stunned expression. "I've decided to get drunk tonight, for the first time in my life." I laughed.

"That's going to be interesting," he said. "You know champagne gets you drunk quickly, right?"

I handed him the bottle for him to open.

"We should play a game," he suggested. "Truth or drink. I ask you a question, and if you don't want to answer, you drink. Simple."

"Right, the easiest games are usually the most dangerous." I played some Maroon 5 on my phone and sat across from him. "What if we just answer everything? No one drinks?"

Sam thought for a moment. "Let's change it to Truth *and* drink then." He popped the cork and took a sip. I settled back on the pillows and put my feet in his lap. "Ready?" He passed me the bottle and started massaging my left foot.

"Okay." I took a drink. "You start."

"What was the last thing you Googled?"

"How to get back to the hotel from the restaurant. What was your most embarrassing moment in public?"

"I fell flat on my ass in front of eighty thousand people," he said, laughing. "It was awful. What's your lucky number and why?"

After each question, the bottle went back and forth between us. We knew this was a terrible idea, but we couldn't stop.

"Seven, and I have no idea why. I've just always liked it. When was the last time you cried, and why?"

He blushed. "When I listened to the song today."

I smiled. "It's a beautiful song."

"You're my inspiration, Lena," he admitted. "As long as I have your support, I know everything will be okay."

It was my turn to blush. Sam smirked and asked his next question.

"How close have you come to cheating on someone?"

"Not close at all," I said. "I can't stand cheating."

"By the way, who was that guy at the restaurant?"

"My turn, Martin."

He rolled his eyes and took a long sip before handing me the bottle.

"He's the marketing manager here. He was trying to convince me to have dinner with him, to 'get to know each other better.' Have you ever used someone else's toothbrush?"

"Yeah, yours."

I frowned. "What do you mean, mine? When?"

"After that first night, when I woke up at your place. I didn't have one, so I used yours."

"Gross!" I threw a pillow at him. "That's disgusting!"

"Oh, come on." He laughed. "Considering what you've put in your mouth, you're really worried about a toothbrush?"

"You're so romantic."

Sam grinned. "Always. What's the most embarrassing thing you've done while drunk?"

"I've never been drunk." I shrugged.

"Seriously? Why?"

"I got married too young and never had a wild phase. To be honest, I'm already feeling a bit dizzy. Let's see how far I can go. What's the biggest age gap you've had with a partner?"

"That's easy. Ten years."

I blinked. "Are you talking about me?"

"Yes. You're the oldest woman I've ever slept with. Congrats, I guess."

"Gee, thanks."

We laughed, both clearly tipsy.

"Who's the most scandalous person you've ever slept with?"

Ha. Here comes revenge.

"You."

"Liar! I'm not scandalous. I'm quiet."

"You're WHAT?" I laughed. "You're ridiculously loud during sex, Sam. I wish I could record you sometime."

"Right. Said the queen of silence who never moans my name loud enough for the neighbours to hear."

I poked him playfully. "I never claimed to be quiet." I grinned. "But you definitely are loud! So, what's the most humiliating thing that's happened to you during sex?"

"Humiliating?" He rubbed his chin, thinking. "I don't think I've ever had an experience like that—at least not one I can recall. Anyway, changing the subject. What's that scar on your shoulder?"

I froze. I thought he hadn't noticed, but how could he not? The scar started at the base of my neck and ran down to my arm—a thin line, but visible up close.

"I fell out of a second-story window and broke my collarbone. I needed surgery, and this is the result. Tell me something you couldn't live without."

"My family," he said with a soft smile. "What's the biggest secret you're keeping from everyone in this room?"

Damn it. I stared at him, feeling the weight of the champagne in my system. I took one last, deep sip. After a few calming breaths, something pushed me to share. Maybe it was bravery—or just the alcohol loosening my tongue.

"I didn't fall from the window. I jumped to escape my ex-husband, who was about to smash a crystal vase over my head."

His eyes widened in shock. "Lena, I… I'm so sorry." He struggled to process what I'd just said. It wasn't a part of my past I ever wanted to revisit. "Is that what you dream about every night?"

"What do you mean?" I asked, my voice barely a whisper. "Do I talk in my sleep?"

"Well, yes," he admitted, looking uncomfortable. "You say things like 'please, don't,' 'don't hurt me,' and 'goodbye, Noah.'"

I dropped the empty bottle onto the bed and covered my face with both hands.

"Hey." Sam moved closer and pulled me against him. My eyes burned, and I felt a knot tightening in my throat. "It's okay. None of it was your fault, Lena."

Even though I knew that, I couldn't stop the flood of tears. I sobbed into his chest, feeling raw and exposed. The memories of those days with Noah rushed back, overwhelming me even after all this time. Sam kissed the top of my head and held me, trying to soothe my trembling body.

"I think I'm drunk," I said, my voice muffled and shaky. "I can't stop crying, and I don't even know why!"

"Oh, God." He chuckled softly. "We've just discovered you're a crying drunk."

I laughed weakly. "Sorry."

He cupped my face and made me look into his eyes. "Never apologize for crying about what happened. It wasn't your fault, and I'll never let you feel like it was. And as for the drunk crying, we've all been there."

Something warm and comforting blossomed inside me. I wasn't sure if it was his steady voice or the concern in his eyes. He cared about me, deeply. I pulled him closer and kissed him, letting the alcohol blur the lines between us. Everything felt hazy, and I knew I'd regret it in the morning, but right now, I just wanted him.

A knock at the door startled us.

"Are you expecting someone?" Sam asked.

"No. Go hide in the bathroom; I'll see who it is."

"What? I'm not hiding in the bathroom!"

"Yes, you are." I disentangled myself from his arms, and as soon as I stood, the room spun. Sam quickly steadied me. "I'm fine. God, how do you do this?"

"Do what?" He looked amused.

"Drink and still manage to walk straight." Sam laughed, and I couldn't help but smile. "Seriously, go to the bathroom. I can't explain why you're in my room at this hour. It's almost…"

"Eight." He glanced at my phone and frowned. "You have sixteen missed calls from an unknown number."

Another knock.

"I'll deal with it later. Just go!"

Reluctantly, Sam slipped into the bathroom and closed the door. I took a deep breath and cracked open the door. My stomach dropped.

"Rento, what are you doing here?"

"Hi, Elena," he slurred, trying to sound sensual but failing miserably. "Can I come in?"

"Um, no." I was both shocked and, honestly, very drunk. "What's going on? What do you want?"

"Marry me?" Rento's smile was crooked, and he reeked of alcohol. "Just marry me, Elena."

His voice was getting louder, and I started to panic. He was clearly more wasted than I was and was making a scene in the hotel hallway.

"Please, let me in." He pushed against the door, and I held firm.

"Rento, you need to go home. I'm not marrying you. I don't even know you!"

He completely misread the situation. After I spoke, he pushed harder and barged into the room, grabbing my wrist.

"Hey! Get out now!"

"I can fuck you, then we'll get to know each other." He tried to drag me further inside, his grip painfully tight. I was furious and stunned at the same time. A man like him couldn't even notice the clothes on the chair beside the bed—another man's clothes.

"Rento, let go of me!" I shouted, but I didn't have to repeat myself. The next second, he was yanked away from me.

"She told you to get the hell out!" Sam's voice echoed in the room as he restrained my colleague. His anger was palpable, and I shivered at the intensity.

"Who the hell are you? What are you doing in my future wife's room?" Rento yelled back.

When I turned to shut him up, the sight was surreal: Rento was flailing wildly, and Sam, with a towel wrapped around his head, was trying not to destroy him. Somehow, Rento broke free and managed to land a punch, splitting the skin above Sam's eyebrow. Sam retaliated, hitting him twice—once in the face, then in the stomach—before throwing him out of the room. All I could do was stand there, wide-eyed.

Sam pulled off the towel and came over to me. "Are you okay?" He checked me over, his face bloody and worried. I let out an involuntary laugh, and his concern deepened.

"Is this what happens when people get drunk? Random guys show up proposing marriage?"

He couldn't help but laugh. "Never happened to me, but they say everyone's different when they're drunk." He kissed my forehead and wrapped me in a hug. "Are you sure you're okay?"

"Yeah," I whispered. "Come on, let's take care of you."

He sat on the bed, grunting as I dabbed at the cut above his eye with the towel. His hands moved up and down my legs, his touch reassuring.

"You looked ridiculous with that towel," I teased. "Like a low-budget western villain."

"I know." He rolled his eyes. "But I'd rather look stupid than let something happen to you. And I know you'd kill me if someone recognized me."

I stroked his cheek gently. "Thank you for saving me."

"You're welcome." He held my hand to his face and smiled when I yawned. "Looks like you're the kind of drunk who gets emotional and sleepy."

"And you're the kind of drunk who's a brave idiot." I rested my head against his.

"We're a perfect match then," he murmured. "You cry and sleep, and I take care of you."

"Deal."

We shared a slow, lingering kiss before he tucked me into bed.

"Sweet dreams, Lena." He kissed my cheek, and I drifted off, surrendering to sleep.

CHAPTER SIX

Elena

DEAR GOD. IT'S ME, ELENA, AGAIN. I SWEAR I'LL NEVER get drunk ever again. This hangover is definitely a punishment from hell after last night.

Sam was moving around the room, and I just wanted him to stop. My head felt like it was about to explode, my stomach was on fire, and I was convinced I'd been hit by a truck. The awful taste in my mouth wasn't helping either. I winced as something clattered to the floor. "For the love of God, Martin," I groaned. "Can't you just sit still? People are dying over here."

He sat down beside me, and I dared to open one eye.

"How are you even alive after last night?"

Sam chuckled. "You really can't handle your booze, can you?" He handed me a glass of orange juice and a painkiller. "This should help."

"Doubt it," I muttered, sinking back into the bed and covering my face with a pillow.

"What time's your flight tomorrow?"

"I have no idea," I grumbled. "I think it's around noon. I'm heading to the airport first thing in the morning."

He kept trying to make conversation, but I couldn't handle it. After the third unanswered question, he finally gave up and settled into the armchair by the window. I cracked open my left eye and smiled faintly. He was holding a notebook, scribbling away. I hoped whatever he was writing would turn into the biggest hit of his career.

"Lena?" A familiar voice called softly. "Hey, beautiful. Time to wake up."

Someone was gently running their fingers through my hair, dropping kisses behind my ear and along my neck.

"Hmm," I groaned. "Go away."

A laugh echoed in the room, and I knew exactly who it was. I mean, of course I knew—it wasn't like there were many options for who else could be in my room. But that laugh, that sweet laugh, confirmed it.

"Wake up. I'm starving, and I don't want to eat alone." Sam's hand was on the back of my neck, kneading it gently.

"If you keep that up, I'll never leave this bed," I murmured, smiling as he kissed my cheek. I sat up, still feeling like I'd been hit by a truck. "What time is it?"

"Almost one in the afternoon. I ordered us some lunch." He gestured to the small table. "Spaghetti with shrimp sauce. I hope you like it."

I dragged myself out of bed and joined him. Sam handed me a plate as I sat down. The food looked incredible and smelled amazing, but I just stared at it.

"What's wrong?" he asked. "Don't you like it? I can order something else."

"No, it's not that." My stomach grumbled in protest. "I'm just not really hungry."

He laughed. "Yeah, I figured. Hangovers suck, eh? Next time we play truth or drink, it'll have to be with orange juice. You know, the drink you, the oh-so-mature grown-up, offered me."

"I'm glad my suffering is so entertaining for you." I rolled my eyes, making him laugh harder.

"You're not suffering, Elena. Try to eat a little; you'll feel better, I promise. I've been there."

After a few minutes of me just picking at the food, Sam scooted his chair closer and took the fork from my hand.

"Open up," he commanded.

"You're not feeding me." This was getting way too intimate, even for us.

"If you're not going to eat on your own, then yes, I am." His tone was insistent. "Come on, Elena. It's just shrimp, not a three-course meal."

"Fine, I'll eat," I muttered. He handed the fork back, but stayed close, watching me. "You're so bossy."

He smirked and kissed my earlobe. "And you're so grumpy. Let's add that to your drunk profile: emotional, sleepy, and grumpy."

I rolled my eyes, and we finished our meal quietly. After brushing my teeth, I climbed back into bed with my laptop. It was Friday, and I still had some work to catch up on. Sam called room service to clear away the dishes, then settled beside me, scribbling in his notebook, hiding the pages from view.

"Working on new songs?" I asked.

"Hopefully," he replied, glancing at me. "What is it?" Sam asked, noticing my expression.

"Nothing. Just worried you might write about something... risky."

He raised an eyebrow. "Worried I'll write a song about our amazing morning sex?"

“Honestly, yes,” I admitted, feeling my cheeks heat up.

Sam thought for a moment. “Would that bother you? I mean, I wouldn’t use your name, obviously, but what about drawing on our... situation for inspiration?”

“I’d rather avoid the risk.” I shrugged. “You could lose your contract, and I’d get fired if anyone found out what’s going on between us. Besides, I think you can do better than writing about the oldest woman you’ve ever been with.”

“Oh, come on.” He shook his head, grinning. “You’re never letting that go, are you?”

“Not a chance.”

“I hate you.”

“No, you don’t.” I batted my eyelashes dramatically. Sam rolled his eyes.

“You’re right.” He kissed me. “I don’t.”

His phone rang, and he reached over to grab it from the bedside table.

“I’ll be right back,” Sam said, giving me a quick wink.

For some godforsaken reason, he decided to leave the room, but not before I heard him greet his father.

It was nearly five in the afternoon when I decided to take a hot bath, hoping to finally wash away the lingering effects of last night’s alcohol. I’d managed to be incredibly productive at work, thanks to being eleven time zones ahead of my coworkers. That left me with the rest of the afternoon and evening free.

I considered going out for a walk, but with Sam around, that wasn’t an option. I couldn’t leave him alone, but I also didn’t want to risk anyone seeing us together. I sighed as I pulled a towel off the hook. Damn it, Martin and his reckless impulsiveness.

When I returned to the bedroom, he was sprawled out on the bed, hands behind his head, eyes following my every move as I got dressed. His gaze made me blush, which was rare. It wasn't that I was insecure about my body—I never had been. Maybe it was because Noah had always been there, and I'd never had to go through the awkwardness of winning someone over. It had just felt natural to be with him. And after our divorce, I had no intention of getting involved with anyone anytime soon, so I didn't really care about how others saw me. I wanted to look and feel good for myself, to prove that I was worthy of this second chance life had given me, even with the scars I'd carry forever. But there was something about the way Sam's eyes lingered on my hips that made me feel like the most desirable woman in the world.

"What are your plans for tonight?" he asked.

"I thought about exploring Tokyo's nightlife," I said, slipping on some sweatpants. "But I'm worried it's too risky. Someone might see you and start asking questions."

He nodded slowly. "Would that be so bad?" he asked, sitting up, his tone cautious. "Being seen with me, I mean."

There it was, his insecurity shining through that perfectly sculpted face of his. I knelt beside him on the bed.

"Sam, it's not that I wouldn't want to be seen with you," I said softly, touching his cheek. He leaned into my hand. "It's just that it could cause us all sorts of problems, and I can't risk that. I've finally got my life back on track, and things are going really well at work. I don't want to lose any more than I already have."

"So you'd rather lose me?" His voice turned cold, and I couldn't help but flinch at his words.

"I don't want to lose anything, Sam. If we can keep this quiet and continue as we are, I'd take that. But if it's too much for you, or if you're looking for something more serious, I understand. You're free to go whenever you need to."

He exhaled sharply, frustration evident. "I thought we were building something real here."

Oh God, not this again. Not now. I closed my eyes, searching for the right words.

"Sam, I wish we'd had a better start. But this is real life, and things don't work out that perfectly." I cupped his face in my hands. "We're in different stages of our lives, and we can't fully enjoy whatever this is while we're both at Icon Records."

"Then I'll leave the label," he said, far too quickly. "Or you could. I don't care. We can figure it out."

"I'm not quitting my job, and that's not how it works for you," I said firmly. "You'd have to pay an absurd fine for breaking your contract, and your career would be over before it even began."

"I don't care, Elena." He jumped off the bed, his voice raw. "I'll pay it. I'll give up everything if it means being with you."

What?

"You're not thinking straight."

"Yes, I am. I'll give up all of this for you. Forever."

"I don't want forever with you!" I practically yelled back. The words flew out before I could stop them. They shouldn't have come out like that, so harsh and sudden, but I couldn't hold back. He wasn't thinking clearly; he was willing to throw away everything for me, and I couldn't handle that. Not for myself, at least. If he wanted to destroy his life, it wouldn't be because of me. We stared at each other, both stunned by my outburst.

"Well, I knew I cared more than you did, but I didn't think..." He shook his head. "What am I to you, Elena?"

"Sam..."

"No," he cut me off, raising a hand. "The truth now. What is this?"

I'd told him he could leave, right? Maybe it was time to burn this bridge.

"I don't love you, Sam. I don't see this going anywhere beyond what we have now. We get along, we have fun, and that's it. I don't want a relationship with you—or anyone, for that matter. It's not you, you're amazing, and the sex is great, but I just like spending time with you. I'm sorry, but you asked for the truth, and that's it."

He stared at me, processing what I'd said before turning and walking out. I tried to stop him, but he needed time, and I couldn't deny him that, not after what I'd just said.

I felt awful for hurting him, but I felt even worse for letting him think there was something more between us. I hadn't been fair to either of us.

I didn't know where he went. I tried calling him a few times before his phone switched off. I was getting dressed to go look for him when he finally walked through the door.

"For fuck's sake, Martin," I yelled. "Where were you?"

"Out." He shrugged, his expression blank.

"Oh, so you chase after me and then vanish without a word? What if something had happened to you? How would I find you?"

He rolled his eyes and sat on the bed. "It's funny, isn't it? You let me in, then tell me I'm nothing to you. We're even."

I moved closer, reaching to touch his hair, but he pulled away.

"You're right." I sighed. "But I'm not ready for this, Sam. I'm not ready for a…"

My phone rang, interrupting me. It was a call from the office in Toronto, so I answered.

"What's up?" I said. "Yeah, why?" Sam started packing his suitcase. I grabbed his arm, silently asking him to wait. He looked at my hand like my touch burned. "Got it. And when did this get decided? How long? Six months? Seriously?" Sam's attention shifted as soon as he heard the timeline. "No, it's fine. I'll handle it. Let's see if we can move the venue around. Just keep me updated, okay? Thanks." I hung up and took a deep breath. "When were you planning to tell me that you're going to California on Tuesday?"

His eyebrows shot up. "Why does that matter to you? Do you even care?"

I shut my eyes and counted to ten.

"I had a photoshoot scheduled for you on Wednesday. So yes, it does matter. Thanks for the heads-up."

"I'm sure you can reschedule," he muttered, zipping up his bag.

"It's not just about the date, Sam! I need new photos; the ones we have are old." He either wasn't listening or was pretending not to. "You know what? Forget it. I'll handle it. I've managed bigger stars; I won't let a spoiled kid get in the way. Victoria can go to California and take some shots of your precious self."

"What? You're not coming?" He sounded surprised.

"What difference does it make?" I snapped back. "Do you even care?"

He glared at me. "And stop calling me a kid!"

"Then stop acting like one!" I shouted.

We stood there, glaring at each other, both breathing hard. Without another word, he grabbed his suitcase and stormed out, muttering about finding another room. His plan fell apart when he learned the hotel was fully booked, and he returned, asking if he could sleep on the couch.

"It's more than you deserve," I muttered.

After calling Vicky to set up her trip to California, I turned in early, counting down the hours until I could head back home and stay the hell away from that stubborn man-to-be.

Sam and I hadn't been on speaking terms since I left the hotel that Saturday. Now, three months after he flew to California, I wished I'd at least said goodbye. Vicky had gone to L.A. as planned and returned with some incredible photos. In the end, his "stupid ass" wasn't that bad after all.

During those months, I realized how lonely it felt to be without him. There was no one I could talk to, no one I could admit that I missed him to. We'd had our ups and downs, but we were mostly good together. We liked the same music, and we both loved omelettes. He even made one once, and I had to admit, it was the best I'd ever had. He'd talk endlessly about his sister, Amelia, a brilliant teenage girl I hadn't met yet. The way his brown eyes lit up when he mentioned her was heartwarming.

I knew Sam had come back to Canada a couple of times during those months, but pride kept us apart and silent. A knock on my door brought me back to reality.

"Sorry to bother you, Lena." Morgana poked her head in, and I gestured for her to come in. "The design team wanted me to let you know they're about to send over the edited photos and the colour palette they've chosen for the new material. There's also a list of TV shows and journalists Vicky and I think would be good for Martin to connect with. We can schedule an appearance on one of the shows or an interview before the album release."

She handed me a stack of papers, and I started to skim through them. "This looks great, Morgs," I said. "But I think we should hold off on some of the interviews until after the first single drops. Keep his name out there, but build a bit of anticipation."

"I'm good with that," she replied with a smile. "We've highlighted the most important ones. Now we just need to narrow it down and figure out the timing."

"Perfect! I'll go over these and check in with his assistant to see if there's anyone specific they want to include."

Just as Morgana was about to respond, my phone rang. It was Jeremy, calling me to his office. I rolled my eyes at his demanding tone and apologized to Morgana. If Jeremy was calling with such urgency, it probably meant there was a crisis brewing.

"Come in," Jeremy called as I knocked on his door.

I froze the moment I stepped inside. Rento was sitting in one of the chairs, that infuriating smirk plastered on his face. "Elena, my dear," he said, crossing the room in an instant and grabbing my hands, kissing each one in turn. Ew. "It's such a pleasure to see you again."

"Right," I muttered, yanking my hands back and moving closer to Jeremy's desk.

"Sorry for calling you in, Elena. I know how busy you are." Jeremy's tone was unusually apologetic, which set off alarm bells. "But it seems our new client was eager to discuss what we can offer for their band here in Canada. They've specifically requested you to create a marketing plan."

"An initial draft, of course," Rento interjected.

"What?" I practically barked, looking from one to the other. "Jer, you know I'm fully committed to the Sam Martin project. I was in a meeting earlier, planning TV spots and interviews for his new album. I can't take on another project right now."

"I know, Elena," Jeremy said with a resigned sigh. "I explained that, but Mr. Yamamoto was quite insistent."

"We agreed to sign with Icon Records to work with the best, Miss Vaughan," Rento added, his voice taking on an unsettling tone as he said my name. "From what I've heard, this company only assigns you and your team when they need top-tier work. You're the best, and we want your expertise to launch our band in Canada."

"Okay, first off, don't call my colleagues 'subordinates,'" I shot back, not bothering to hide my irritation. "They're talented, hardworking professionals who deserve the utmost respect. Second, I simply don't have the bandwidth for this right now. I'd love to help, but my team is tied up with two of the label's biggest projects for the next two years. We can recommend another team who'd do a fantastic job."

"Well." Rento sat back down, his smirk growing. "It looks like we'll need to revisit the contract or perhaps consider terminating it if we can't get the best team on board. That was the agreement we signed in Japan."

Jeremy sighed deeply.

"Jer, you can't do this," I warned him.

"I'm sorry, Lena," he said, looking genuinely pained. Rento, on the other hand, looked elated. "You'll need to delegate some of your responsibilities. We need this marketing plan finalized in two weeks."

Before I could even respond, Rento was already on the phone, gloating to his colleagues in Japan about the "good news."

CHAPTER SEVEN

Elena

I. WAS. WRECKED.

Saying I wasn't feeling great was an understatement. When my alarm blared that Wednesday, my head felt like it was about to explode, every muscle in my body ached, and shivers ran down my spine each time I tried to move. These damned meetings were taking a toll on me, making it feel like I'd been hit by a truck every single day. It had been a week and a half of juggling the Japanese band's endless demands and the SM Project, trying to do everything at once. I wasn't eating properly, barely sleeping, and I hadn't gone out with my team for a drink in ages. My social life was non-existent because the time left to finish that goddamn project was running out.

And yeah, I know what you're thinking—they shouldn't have been my problem. I hadn't agreed to handle their band's marketing, for crying out loud! But Jeremy was determined to keep the clients happy at any cost. I either took it on, or I'd be thrown under the bus.

Today, we had a meeting with Sam and his team, and I had to be there. Even though things were tense between us personally, his career was more than just another project for me. It was my priority. I'd promised myself that I would help make him a household name—and I intended to do just that, no matter what. Regardless of where we stood, Sam had a special place in my heart, and I couldn't let him down by giving anything less than my best.

But the moment I tried to get out of bed, I barely made it to the bathroom before I was throwing up everything from the night before. And that wasn't much to begin with.

I ended up sitting on the cold bathroom floor, tears streaming down my face. I wasn't even sure why I was crying so much, but it felt impossible to stop. Growing up was a bitch, and I just wanted to be ten years old again and at home with my parents. Then I realized that when I was ten, Sam was still a baby, and that made it all feel even worse. I sobbed uncontrollably for what felt like forever before I finally mustered up the energy to drag myself back to bed. I called the office, told them I was sick, and then pulled the covers up over my head. I just wanted to disappear for a while and come back to life when I felt human again.

"His agent didn't seem too bothered, but Mr. Martin wasn't pleased you missed the meeting," Matt was updating me over the phone about what had gone down that day. It was almost 7 p.m., and I was still in bed, feeling like I was on death's doorstep. "But overall, it went smoothly, and they're on board with our ideas."

"Great," I tried to reply, but my voice was barely a whisper. I was hoping to wake up feeling better, not worse. "But Matt, we still need to nail down that centrepiece—the rose. It has to be something so unique that when people see a photo, they instantly think of Sam's concert or his album. It needs to be iconic."

"I get it. I've already talked to the design team about the flowers and the giant rose, but I'm not sure yet. I mean, how can we decide when we don't even know the final direction of the music? Sure, roses are versatile, but what if the sound goes darker? Are we going to use a black rose? That would be a bit much."

"Way too much." That's when I sensed him. I looked over at my bedroom door, and there he was, standing there in shock. "Matt, I've got to go. Thanks for everything today. You're amazing, and I'm so grateful to have you on my team."

"No problem, Lena! Let me know if you need anything. Take care, okay?"

"Thanks. Bye!" I hung up.

"Jesus," Sam whispered.

"Hey." I gave him a small smile, my heart pounding in my chest. God, he looked so… mature and different. "How did you get in here?"

"I knocked, but you didn't answer. I tried calling, but you didn't pick up. So, I tried the door, and surprise—it was unlocked."

"Oh." That was a wake-up call. I'd been so exhausted last night that I hadn't even locked the door. Not my smartest move.

"Yeah, 'oh.' What's going on with you?" Sam sat beside me, placing the back of his hand on my forehead. His touch was cool. "I think you've got a fever."

"I woke up like this. I'm sorry I missed the meeting. I tried, but I barely made it out of the bathroom." I attempted to sit up, but Sam gently pushed me back down. "Thanks for coming anyway. I wanted to say goodbye before I died."

He laughed softly. "You're not dying, Elena. Stop saying that every time you feel terrible. You probably just have the flu. You'll feel better after a shower and some food. I'm here to take care of you, as always."

Sam kissed my forehead and disappeared into my bathroom. I heard him rummaging through the cabinets and drawers. When he came back, he looked determined.

“Come on, time to get up and get some water on you.” He pulled the covers off me, ignoring my groans of protest. Without a word, he lifted me in his arms and carried me to the bathroom.

“I love how you smell.” I nuzzled his neck, inhaling deeply. He smiled.

“Promise me you’ll ignore everything I say today. I’m not even close to being myself.”

“No promises, remember?” he said, his voice teasing but gentle. “The only thing I can promise is that I’m staying until you’re better, and don’t even think about kicking me out.”

He set me down and started undressing me. I could barely keep my eyes open, but I saw the worry etched on his face. I reached up and touched his cheek, and he kissed my hand. Our eyes met, and he gave me a small grin.

“Shower with me?” I asked softly.

“Obviously. You can hardly stand, let alone shower by yourself. And I’m not letting you fall.”

I must have drifted in and out during the shower. I had vague memories of Sam washing my hair and body, then wrapping me in a towel. The next thing I knew, I was back in bed, clean pajamas on, tucked in up to my chin.

“Thank you,” I whispered, holding his hand to keep him close. “Looks like you’re officially my hero. Always taking care of me.”

“I’ll always take care of you, Lena.” Sam brushed his fingers gently across my face. “Even when you shut me out for months, I’ll still be here, waiting for when you need me.”

It was a little unsettling to hear, but also incredibly comforting. In that moment, I couldn’t remember why we’d gone so long without speaking. All I knew was that I’d missed Sam Martin. I missed his laugh when I’d say something silly or the way his brow would furrow when he was concerned. I’d been trying to start fresh, build a new life away from the last nine years, but when Sam looked at me like I mattered, I realized just how much I'd been missing. With those thoughts swirling around, I fell asleep, feeling light and safe for the first time in a long while.

Once, Elena asked if I loved her. I could've sworn I saw a flicker of hope in her eyes, even though she'd never admit it. But I knew that if I'd said anything close to "I love you," she would've walked away. And I couldn't bear the thought of losing her.

Love. What I felt for her went beyond that word. Love was strong, but Elena was everything. She was the feeling I didn't know I was missing. Her laugh was my favourite song. I could give up singing forever, but I couldn't imagine spending another day without her. I still couldn't believe I'd spent my birthday away from her. I hadn't gone far—just to my parents' place—but I'd been too proud to call. It cost me a talk with my dad, and his advice threw me. I'd expected him to tell me to forget her, but instead, he said if Elena was what I wanted, I had to fight for her.

I knew the risks and the judgment, but I didn't care. All I wanted was her. She was my everything. She knew how to calm my anxiety and keep me grounded. Her quick comebacks could drive me crazy, but they also opened my eyes to things I'd never thought about. It was like being slapped and kissed at the same time. I didn't need anyone else's approval as long as I had Elena beside me.

When she told me she'd jumped out of a second-story window to escape her ex, my heart clenched. All I wanted was to hunt that guy down and make him pay for hurting her. Even though I hadn't known her then, the thought of someone that close to her made my blood boil. I wanted to hurt him, to make him suffer for every mark he left on her perfect body.

A soft sound escaped her lips, and I immediately moved closer. Seeing her like this—so fragile and worn out—killed me. I'd trade places with her in a heartbeat. I just wanted her to open those big, beautiful eyes and give me a smile.

"Lena?" I whispered. "How are you feeling?"

No response. She was deep in sleep, just like she'd been for hours. I wanted her to eat, but I couldn't bring myself to wake her. Something was off, and I didn't know what it was. I'd seen bad flus before—my sister almost ended up in the hospital once and slept an entire day fighting it. I hoped that was all this was. But it felt like more than just being sick. She looked drained, with dark circles under her eyes and weight loss that made her cheeks look hollow. Her hips weren't as curvy as before. Something was stressing her out, and it was taking a toll.

This is all your fault, you left her alone, exposed to the world, my anxiety tried to whisper, but I pushed it down. Elena needed me, and I couldn't fall apart now. I grabbed my backpack, took out my notebook and a pen, and settled beside her on the bed, leaning against the headboard with my legs stretched out in front of me. I started writing, not even realizing when I drifted off.

My chest felt tight, and it was hard to breathe. I opened my eyes, confused, and realized Elena was practically draped over me. Her head rested on my neck, her hair tangled across my face, and one of her legs was wedged between mine. My arm was pinned under her, making it almost impossible to get up without waking her. Well, impossible, really.

I touched her forehead and exhaled in relief. Her fever had finally broken. Now, I just had to convince my stubborn girl to eat something and talk about whatever was weighing on her. Talking would help her clear her head and focus on getting better. And I needed to know she was okay before flying to Jamaica to wrap up recording the last few songs for the album.

She murmured my name, and I couldn't help but smile.

"Good morning, beautiful," I whispered when her eyes met mine. "Feeling better?"

She frowned, looking around as if trying to remember where she was. To my disappointment, she pulled away, shifting to her side of the bed and leaving my arms empty.

"Yeah, I guess," she replied hesitantly. "My head still hurts, and my throat's sore, but I'm feeling better. I can't remember much from yesterday, though. I remember talking to Matt on the phone, then you showed up… The rest is kind of a blur."

I found my notebook and pen tucked under the blankets. I'd been writing when she fell asleep on top of them. Setting them aside on the bedside table, I turned to face her, propping myself up on my elbow. She was staring blankly at the ceiling, looking distant. I touched her cheek, and she closed her eyes.

"When I got here, you were talking to Matt about the meeting," I said softly. "Then I made you take a shower to bring your fever down, and when you got back to bed, you crashed. You've been out for twelve hours straight."

"Wow," she murmured. "I didn't even know I could sleep that long."

"Who would've thought? Elena Vaughan, the most morning person ever, sleeping for twelve hours straight. I think you might be getting old," I teased, and she stuck her tongue out at me before smiling—a real, genuine smile that sent warmth rushing through my chest. "Can I kiss you?"

She looked at me in disbelief and laughed. "You shouldn't ask a woman if you can kiss her, Martin." She gave me a mock serious look. "And besides, I'm still sick. I could pass it on to you, and that wouldn't be good."

“Right now, I don’t care about that,” I said, holding her wrists gently when she tried to move away. I just needed to know we were okay, at least somewhat. “I just want you.”

Her eyes softened for a moment, and I took the chance. As our lips met, Elena let out a small, contented sound that was the sweetest thing I’d heard in months. No hit song could ever compare to that.

I kissed her slowly, savouring the moment. Our tongues moved together, our breathing deepened, and I didn’t want it to end. If I died right then, I’d be the happiest guy in the world. It was pure bliss, just solidifying how she was everything to me.

I let go of her wrists, and her hands immediately tangled in my hair, sending shivers down my spine. Before I knew it, she was on top of me, biting my lower lip, her breasts brushing against my chest.

“Hold up, hottie,” I said, gently pushing her back by the shoulders, making her sit on my stomach.

“What?” she whined, her eyes dark with desire, lips red and swollen. I grinned, loving the sight of her like this. “Come on, Martin. It’s been forever.”

“I know,” I chuckled. God, I knew. I’d been counting the days, dreaming of this moment. “But I’m here to take care of you, not to take advantage. We’ll have plenty of time for this. But first, I need you to eat something and talk to me. I can tell something’s bothering you, and I want to help.”

“Does the order matter?” she grumbled, crossing her arms. “I mean, you’re gonna have your way with me eventually. Why can’t we start there?”

I laughed out loud. She was wild, and I loved her for it. “Yeah, it matters to me!” I sat up, keeping my arms around her. Our noses touched, and I saw a hint of a smile on her lips. I pulled her closer, her legs settling around me. “And for someone who didn’t want to kiss me a minute ago, you’ve changed your mind pretty fast.”

“Did I mention I hate you today?” she asked, then kissed me quickly.

"No, you don't hate me," I teased back. "I'm your favourite teenage celebrity, and you can't live without me."

"Ugh, I think I might puke." She climbed off my lap, and I panicked.

"Are you feeling sick?" I asked, moving closer. "Do you need to go to the hospital?"

"No, Martin," she snapped. "You're so sweet, I think I'm going to puke a rainbow."

My jaw dropped. "You're the worst person ever!" I cried out, mock offended. "Here I am, worried about you, and you're making fun of me. I should go back to California and never speak to you again."

She laughed, throwing her head back. "Go ahead, Martin. And if you're not going to have your way with me, go get us some breakfast. I'm starting to get hungry." She blew me a kiss and headed to the bathroom, locking the door behind her and leaving me standing there, smiling like the fool I was.

I'll admit, I wasn't prepared for this. When Elena told me she was hungry, I thought I'd just raid her kitchen and whip something up. But staring blankly at her empty fridge, I realized I had no clue what to do.

She's always been so particular about her groceries, so it was shocking to see nothing there. I knew she liked to hit up Whole Foods on Wednesdays, something about fresh produce, but with her feeling like crap, it made sense she hadn't gone. Her fridge must have been empty for days.

I headed back to the bedroom and heard the shower running. I didn't want to bother her, so I grabbed my wallet, sunglasses, a cap, and my backpack and set off for her favourite market. As soon as I stepped outside, I felt the chill. Winter was creeping in, and Toronto was starting to feel cold and grey again.

Whole Foods wasn't far, but halfway there, I realized just how many bags I'd be hauling back. I should've driven instead of leaving my car parked on her street. The cashier gave me a suspicious look, like she knew who I was but was trying not to show it. I flashed her an honest smile and thanked her for not making a scene.

Walking back with six plastic bags in each hand—yeah, I forgot the reusable ones, sue me—was brutal. My fingers were frozen, and I hadn't even zipped up my jacket. The wind was ruthless, blasting through me and turning my hair into a mess. But I was on a mission, and nothing was stopping me.

"For fuck's sake, why do we live in such a freezing city?" I grumbled as I dropped the bags on the kitchen counter. "Seriously, why not Vancouver? At least their winters are a little more humane."

Elena was sitting on a stool by the island, holding a mug in her hands. "You know you could've just made scrambled eggs and coffee, right? You didn't have to go to Whole Foods."

I stood in front of her and took a sip of her coffee. "Do you really think eggs and coffee would satisfy this six-foot-two body?" I teased. She laughed, and I felt a surge of warmth. "Besides, you've lost weight, and I'm worried you're not eating properly. So, spill what's been going on while I cook you the best breakfast you've ever had."

I started unloading the bags, setting out ingredients for pancakes, eggs, grilled ham, and toast. I was determined to make a proper meal. I heard her sigh and knew she was debating whether or not to open up. I gave her time, and eventually, she spoke.

"Remember that guy from Japan—the one who barged into my room?"

I clenched my jaw. "Yeah, *our* room. What about him?"

"He showed up in Toronto a couple of weeks ago, demanding that I handle his band's marketing. He threatened Jeremy, saying he'd terminate the contract if I wasn't leading the team immediately."

"What?" I whipped around to look at her. "But you're working on my project... And, Lena, don't get me wrong, I've seen what you're doing with my album and the tour. It's incredible, but I know it's taking up all of your time and your team's. How can you handle two projects at once? You're amazing, but that's insane."

"Tell me about it." She looked exhausted. "I told Jer I didn't have time for another project. Your campaign runs until the end of 2019. We have to plan every step, adjusting for feedback from critics and fans. After that, I'm already committed to another major project. I'm already stretched thin, trying to balance both. But when Rento brought up the fine we'd have to pay, Jeremy caved and gave me two weeks to deliver the initial plan."

"That's ridiculous," I fumed.

I was just about to start cooking when she joined me at the stove. I kissed the top of her head, and she gave me a faint smile.

"The past few days have been hell. I couldn't push your project aside, but I still had to draft a plan for the Japanese band. I've been working non-stop, barely sleeping." Her voice cracked. "I think my body just gave out yesterday."

"I never thought I'd say this, but I'm glad it did. At least it forced you to slow down."

I was furious. That asshole Rento had crossed a line, pushing Elena like this. And Jeremy? I was pissed at him too, for making her work herself to the bone. And me? I was mad at myself for not being there when she needed me. I'd been in California, but I could've at least called more often, been a better support.

"I could snap back at you right now, but I know you're right. I'm relieved it happened too. At least now I'll look a bit better when I present the marketing plan tomorrow."

I leaned against the counter, watching her closely. "I'm sorry I wasn't here for you," I murmured. "Maybe I couldn't have done much, but at least I'd have known what was going on. I could've cooked for you or made sure you ate."

Elena set down the last pancake and turned off the stove. When she looked at me, there was something different in her eyes, something I couldn't quite read.

"We weren't speaking," she reminded me with a shrug.

"Why?" I asked quietly.

"Because you're stubborn and can't accept our limits. You act like it's no big deal for us to be seen together, like people wouldn't notice."

"You overthink it. Our personal lives are just that—personal." I pulled her close, wrapping my arms around her shoulders. She hugged me back, resting her head on my chest.

"I'm trying to protect both of us, Sam. We've worked too hard to risk it all. It wouldn't be fair to either of us to lose everything we've built." She tilted her head up, her eyes locking with mine. "Please try to understand. If you can't keep this quiet, the only way we can move forward is apart. I've already blurred the lines by making your project personal. I'm pushing myself and my team harder than ever. Don't ask for more than I can give right now. It's all I've got."

I glanced up, silently begging for some kind of sign. I took a deep breath and closed my eyes.

"You've given me love, then taken it back / Let me taste you and hold you / then out of nowhere, just pain, you turned your back." I sang, feeling her whole body shake with laughter.

"Stop using your songs to mess with me," she teased. When I looked down, Elena had that smile—the one I loved the most. It lit up her whole face, lifting her cheeks and making her eyes crinkle at the corners.

"I love that you know all my lyrics."

She rolled her eyes. "It's called research, Martin."

"Sure, let's go with that." I kissed her forehead. I wanted to say I loved her, that I was completely obsessed with her, but I knew it wouldn't go well.

"Let's finish breakfast. You still owe me a round of wild sex, and I'm not letting you off the hook!" She pulled away and went back to the stove, effortlessly brushing off any talk about us, like she always did.

But right then, I didn't care. If keeping things secret was the only way I could have her, I was fine with it. Someone once said that a little bit is better than nothing at all, and I couldn't agree more.

CHAPTER EIGHT

Elena

I HAD NO IDEA WHAT WAS GOING ON WITH ME. EVER since my marriage ended, I'd sworn off any kind of commitment, determined to focus on my career and myself. It had been the perfect opportunity to break some old habits and put my life back on track.

Then a nineteen-year-old came along and turned everything upside down, leaving me crying on the couch after saying goodbye. Sam was on his way to Jamaica to finish his album, and I was at home, missing him already. And he'd only been gone for twenty minutes! The worst part? I knew he'd be back in a couple of weeks, just in time for Christmas and his sister's graduation. There was absolutely no reason for me to feel like this.

We'd spent most of the weekend together. When he wasn't visiting his parents, he was at my place, showing me pictures and asking for my opinion on how to decorate his new apartment.

I glanced at the time on my phone—5:30 a.m. on a Thursday, and I couldn't go back to sleep. I decided to make a cup of the tea Sam had bought for us to try. When I got to the kitchen, I found a note on the counter.

Don't forget to eat and try not to miss me too much! SM

Honestly, if there was a contest for the sweetest person, Sam would win, no doubt. He was so caring, always putting everyone else's needs before his own. His fans, his family, his friends—they all came first. And for the first time, I felt both full and empty inside. Full of love and gratitude for him, for how he brought a new kind of joy and excitement into my life. Empty because I knew we'd never be able to live our relationship to its fullest. He was young, free, travelling the world, meeting new people, and discovering new things. Someday, he'd meet a girl his age who could keep up with all his adventures, someone without a messy past weighing her down.

And I'd just go on with my life, dealing with my own issues, working hard—both professionally and mentally—to get over him. All I could hope was that he'd look back on our time together with fondness.

I filled the kettle and leaned against the kitchen counter—the same one where we'd had sex for the first time. I grinned at the memory, biting my lip. Things between us had started with a misunderstanding, leading to him singing and practically stalking me around town. Then we'd ended up in bed, again and again, until I'd lost count. We'd had some heated arguments too—he was stubborn and, at times, maddeningly immature. But he brought a breath of fresh air into my life.

The kettle clicked, signalling the water was ready. I poured it into a mug and added the tea bag, then heard a ping from my phone. I walked over to the couch and picked it up.

I know I told you not to miss me, but I miss you already.

I smiled at the screen.

For fuck's sake, Martin! You left half an hour ago! —_—'

Of course, I'd never tell him about the tears or how much I wished he'd turn around and come back. That would freak him out and ruin everything too soon.

I know you miss me too! I'll see you in a few weeks. XX

I pouted at the message but didn't reply. Instead, I took a long, hot shower and got ready for work.

"Is it wrong to be this excited about the party?" Vicky asked, practically bouncing as we grabbed lunch at the cafeteria.

I couldn't help but laugh.

"Well, since I rarely see you this hyped, I'd say it's great to see you so happy," I teased. "I only glanced at the invite. Where's it happening again? Is there a theme?"

"You're joking, right?" She stared at me, disbelief written all over her face.

"Uh, no?"

Victoria rolled her eyes. "Sam Martin is performing, Lena! He's one of three artists doing a pocket show at the Icon Records gala!"

I nearly choked on my coffee, scalding my tongue. Damn it, why was this stuff always so hot?

"But he's still so new," I managed, after swallowing. "We usually see industry legends at the gala. How did they end up inviting him?"

"No clue, but I'm proud of him. He's part of our team, and we should celebrate that, right?"

I was about to respond when my phone rang. Seeing an unknown number, I knew exactly who it was. I told Vicky I'd catch up with her at the office, and she left.

"Hello?" I answered, moving to the farthest table in the cafeteria.

"Hey, Lena." Sam's voice filled my ear, and I closed my eyes for a second. "Did you hear? I'm performing at the Icon Records gala!"

I could hear the surprise in his voice, and I smiled. "Actually, I just found out. But congratulations! This is huge—you know that, right?"

"Yeah, I guess..." His uncertainty was almost palpable.

"It *is* huge! And I'm so proud of you."

"Really?" He sounded genuinely shocked. What was up with him?

"Absolutely. The whole team is thrilled and can't wait for the party!"

"Thanks! I have to go; my flight's boarding. I'll call you when I land, okay?"

"Okay! Safe travels." And come back safe, I almost added but hung up before I could embarrass myself.

The silence didn't last long. On my way back to the office, my phone rang again—this time, it wasn't Sam.

"John!" I practically shouted with relief.

"What the hell, Elena?" he barked, but I could tell he was trying not to laugh. "I've been working for *months* trying to get my top artist a spot at this damn party. Then you swoop in with your barely legal protégé and snag a gig for him?"

I threw my head back, laughing. "Only the strong survive, John!" I joked. "My boy's got serious talent. Hard to compete with those falsettos."

"You've got to be kidding me. He's still practically a kid and already causing me headaches. I guess the only way I can secure a spot like that is to lure you to New York."

"In your dreams, my friend." I couldn't stop smiling. Talking to John always brightened my day, his voice somehow both calming and exciting, much like Sam's. "But you didn't call just to praise my unmatched skill in turning newbies into stars, did you?"

"Well, that too, but I actually called to ask if you'd be my date to the gala."

I froze when I spotted Rento hovering by my office door. "Hang on a sec, John," I whispered, pulling the phone away from my ear. "Our meeting's not until 10 a.m., right?"

I had no desire to deal with him, but he didn't seem to get the hint.

"Who are you talking to?" John's voice came through the phone, but I ignored him.

"I know," Rento murmured, looking a bit nervous. "I just thought I'd ask if you'd go to the gala with me. You've probably just received the invitation, so I'm guessing no one else has asked you yet."

"Wrong," John called out from the phone, and I stifled a laugh.

"Sorry, Rento, but I already have a date." I put the phone back to my ear. "I'd love to go with you, John."

I walked past Rento and into my office, John's laughter echoing through the phone, making me smile even wider.

It had been a day packed with meetings with my incredible team. The SM Project was nearly finished and ready to launch. We'd decided that May 2018 would be our lucky month, and all the pre-launch interviews, photoshoots, and public appearances were lined up. Sam would be busy after Christmas, travelling from city to city and even to different countries to promote his third album, but we were all thrilled. When it came time to pick the first single from the three songs we had, I admit I cheated a bit. With my phone hidden under the table, I texted Sam.

If I told you it would make me really happy if the song you showed me at the hotel that day were the first single, would you say that's the one you want?

His reply almost made me smile.

I can't believe Miss "We-Can't-Do-This" is really doing this!

I wrote back:

Please? They're about to ask for your choice. I love that song, and I have a strong feeling it'll be a huge hit!

My phone buzzed again, and I exhaled in relief.

Yes, Lena. I'll tell them that one has to be the single. But you owe me.

Before putting my phone away, I replied:

Can't wait to pay it back. Xx

The artwork from the Design team was also incredible! Our biggest concern was making sure the flowers matched the new songs, but when we spoke with Sam and his manager, they both assured us it would be perfect (Alex replied to my email; Sam texted me). I also managed to finalize the last details with the Japanese band, and the only thing left was to present it. After that, according to Jeremy, I'd be free. I wasn't sure I trusted him, but I was determined to step back from this project. I'd go as far as getting a doctor's note citing high stress levels if I had to.

The gala was on Friday, so I decided to find a new dress after work. I didn't want to spend too much, so I wandered around Eaton Centre, hoping to find something within my budget. Even though my usual style is more casual—ballet flats, jeans, and T-shirts—I wanted something stunning. And then I saw it, in a shop window whose name I couldn't recall. The sparkle and long sleeves drew me in, but it was the back that truly shocked me when I got closer.

"Can I try that dress?" I asked the shopkeeper. She must have seen the excitement in my eyes because she smiled brightly and led me to the dressing rooms, handing me the dress.

Everything about it was perfect; it felt like it was made just for me. At first glance, it seemed classic: black, with a boat neckline and a slightly slim fit, adorned with sequins from top to bottom and on both sleeves.

It hugged my curves, the mermaid silhouette skimming down my legs and highlighting my not-so-modest behind. But the back... oh, the back was something else. The fabric ended just where my shoulders and arms met, plunging all the way down, leaving my entire back exposed. It stopped only three fingers above my butt. With every movement, the gown sparkled, but it was nothing compared to how it made me feel.

My first thought was how Noah would have reacted. He would never have let me wear something like this. If he was in a good mood, he'd say it wasn't suitable for a decent, married woman. In a bad mood, his comments would be far worse. Remembering that, I started to undress, but then I stopped. Noah wasn't around anymore, and I wasn't that woman anymore. I was in control of my life, had a successful career at Icon Records, and paid my own bills. I could even say I had a decent relationship with another man.

Without a second thought, I slipped the dress back on and smiled at the reflection. I felt powerful, sexy, and confident. The way the soft fabric clung to my body made me feel invincible and unbreakable.

Even though it cost more than I'd planned, I bought the dress. It was a gift to the new, liberated Elena, the one who survived an abusive marriage and was finally moving on. I left the store feeling almost euphoric. Instead of heading home, I browsed for some shoes and accessories. Passing by a high-end furniture store, I spotted a huge L-shaped couch that I knew someone would love. I snapped a photo and sent it to Sam.

Found this couch at Eaton Centre! I think it'd look great in your living room, near the windows.

The advantage of being only one hour ahead was that I didn't have to wait long for a response.

Wow, that thing is massive! It could probably eat a person whole! Could you check if it's comfortable and ask for the dimensions, please? And what are you doing at Eaton?

I ignored his last question. It wasn't his business what I was or wasn't doing. Instead of answering, I went into the store. A cheerful salesperson approached me, and I asked about the couch, sitting down to test it out. Honestly, it was more comfortable than I'd imagined.

It's so comfy I could live on this couch! And the guy says it's a contemporary design, whatever that means.

Seconds later, he texted back.

Decision made. That's our couch. I'll have the office handle it. Thanks! <3

Sam's team and the salesperson handled the details. They discussed payment and delivery, and I realized how practical—and boring—celebrity life could be. Picking out furniture should be fun, right? Going to the store, testing things out, imagining them in your space. But for celebrities, all it took was a call and it was done. Cold, distant, weird. But it wasn't my problem or my couch, so I shouldn't care, right?

A little later, I bought some black heels and accessories. Then that familiar number popped up on my screen again.

"How mad would you be if I told you I got you a gift?" Sam's voice was both anxious and nervous.

"Well, hello! Yes, I'm doing great, thanks for asking. I'm glad you're okay too," I teased.

"Elena." His grumble made me smile.

"I don't know. Probably very mad. But tell me what you bought, and I'll decide."

He hesitated, and I rolled my eyes. If you know someone will be upset, why do it anyway?

"I got you a pair of earrings," he murmured. "They're simple, but since I'm sure you won't go to the gala with me, I wanted to be there with you in some way."

I almost rolled my eyes at how sweet he was.

"Right." I took a moment to process. Why did everyone suddenly want to go to this gala with me? "Well, thank you, I guess. And you'll be there too, it's not like we won't see each other."

"Yeah." I could almost hear him smiling. "But you won't be there as my date. So I thought this would be a way to go with you without actually being with you. You're not taking anyone, right?"

I bit my lower lip. "See, about that... I do have a date." He exhaled sharply. "And I can't wait to introduce you two. He's amazing; you'll see."

Silence. I glanced at the screen to make sure I hadn't lost the connection.

"Still there?" I asked, and he chuckled.

"I love how you avoid using my name, just in case."

I rolled my eyes. "I hate you."

"I don't." Those simple words sent shivers down my spine. "Call me Philip or Romeo, Elena. Those are my other names. Just promise me you're not going with Rento, or I swear I'll shove these earrings down his throat."

I grimaced. "God, no. He tried to ask me, but my date beat him to it. I wasn't available when that piece of trash tried."

"Good. I hope you have a great time at the gala," he said, his voice tinged with sadness.

"I hope we both do."

I kept walking for a bit longer so we could keep talking before I had to head to the subway. I missed him—his humour, his easy laughter. I couldn't wait to have Sam back in town in a few days.

I completely nailed the Japanese band's presentation. Everything went even better than I'd hoped, and when they mentioned keeping me on the project, Jeremy finally stepped in and confirmed that my part was done. They got what they wanted—the best employee in the company to create a marketing plan for their band. Now, I could pass it on to another team and get back to my life. Rento's disappointment was obvious, and I felt like dancing on the table, I was so thrilled.

After the meeting, I decided to take the stairs instead of the elevator in our nine-story building. I heard my phone ring and checked the message:

I'm home!

I stumbled a bit and nearly fell, grabbing the banister just in time to keep my phone from flying out of my hand. My heart raced as I considered my options. I could head straight over and stop missing him, or I could pretend to be focused on work and meet Sam later at his new place.

I'll be there soon!

I stopped by Jeremy's office and told him I wasn't feeling well. He was in a good mood, so he told me to go home, rest, and enjoy the success of the presentation. I let my team know I'd be out until Monday and left. When I reached the building's lounge, another message popped up.

There's a car waiting for you outside.

It felt like a scene from a movie. One of his security team members got out of the car when he saw me and opened the door. He couldn't hide his satisfied smile, and I just nodded before getting in. We exchanged a few words before he dropped me off at the garage of a sleek building, seventeen minutes after leaving Icon Records. I took the elevator and entered the code for the top floor. The ride felt like forever, and I thought I might faint. My heart was hammering so loudly I was sure the whole building could hear it. Never in my life had I imagined I'd be doing something like this. Realizing I'd left work early just to see Sam made me laugh nervously. It was ridiculous, reckless, and impulsive, but so thrilling that I didn't care about the potential fallout. I just wanted to be with him.

The elevator stopped on the tenth floor, and when the doors opened, I took a deep breath and stepped out. It felt like being in a hotel—long white corridors with grey carpeting and doors on either side. I walked to his apartment, hesitating in front of the grey door with red accents and the apartment number in crisp white. The modern design was intimidating, and I almost turned back, but my hand moved on its own and knocked. Sam opened the door with a smile.

"Welcome," he said, pulling me inside and closing the door behind us.

I looked around in awe. The apartment was enormous, probably three times bigger than my house. The entryway led to a spacious open floor plan with sleek laminated flooring that stretched as far as I could see, perfectly complementing the grey walls. The ceiling had plaster moulding with recessed lights in all the right places. Beyond the entryway was what seemed to be a bedroom, while to the right was a small closet with sliding doors, designed for winter coats. Sam took my coat and hung it up, then handed me a pair of loafers so I could get comfortable. A few steps further, we were in a sleek L-shaped kitchen, right next to the closet. An island with two stools stood in the centre, perfect for quick meals. The cabinets were a deep, elegant brown, contrasting beautifully with the beige quartz countertops. Two of the upper cabinets had frosted glass, adding a modern touch to the warm wood. The fridge was seamlessly integrated, hidden behind large doors, and the rest of the appliances were stainless steel. I held my breath when I saw the cooktop—something I'd always dreamed of having. Across from the kitchen was a small dining area with floor-to-ceiling windows and a spacious balcony.

The whole apartment was open-concept, with walls only for the bedroom and bathroom, leaving the rest of the space wide and free. I smiled when I spotted the white couch I'd picked out in the corner of the living room.

"You were right," Sam said, taking my hand and intertwining our fingers, making my heart skip a beat. That small gesture made me feel protected, like nothing else mattered but us. "It's the perfect size and so freaking comfortable! If I hadn't already bought a bed, I'd sleep on it forever."

The couch was near another floor-to-ceiling window with a stunning view. Sam led me to the opposite side and pointed out one of Toronto's most famous landmarks: the CN Tower.

He opened the window, and a cool breeze swept over my face. I leaned against the railing and took in the city I'd made my home. Sam wrapped his arms around me from behind and kissed my ear softly. I closed my eyes, smiling like an idiot, feeling chills run through me. "You have an amazing view," I murmured.

"I know," he said, his gaze still on me.

I rolled my eyes. "I'm talking about the city, not me, Martin," I grumbled, and he grinned.

"Right now, you're what makes this view worthwhile."

I looked into his eyes and sighed. The depth in his gaze pulled me in like he could see straight into my soul. Not wanting to waste another second, he turned me to face him and pressed me against the window, his hands cradling my face. Our lips met, and I couldn't hold back the longing I'd felt in his absence. Words couldn't describe how much I wanted things to be different, how much I wished we could be together without complications. When he held my hand, everything made sense. It felt like all the struggles I'd faced had led me to him. Nothing else mattered—not the judgment we'd face, not our fears, not even the age difference. I just wanted him—always him, and nothing more.

Our kiss was intense, filled with desire and need. His hands moved from my face, exploring my body, gripping, stroking, and pulling me closer. It was the longest, most intense kiss we'd ever shared, overflowing with… love? I pushed the thought away, deciding not to build up expectations. When we finally paused for breath and looked at each other, we both started laughing. His lips were swollen and red, and he was breathing heavily. I probably looked the same—or maybe worse, with my heart pounding so loudly it felt like it was playing its own drum solo.

I pulled him by his shirt and rested my forehead against his chest. Sam held me close. "Has your bed been delivered?" I asked, biting my lip, craving him in every way.

He laughed. "They're supposed to bring it by the end of the day. But we have the couch."

I glanced at the couch beside us and smiled. "It is beautiful, isn't it? I have great taste in furniture. You're welcome."

"Yeah, it's perfect. But it'll look even better with you lying on it, completely naked," he whispered in my ear, making me shiver.

He lifted me effortlessly, and I wrapped my legs around his waist. We kissed again, deeper this time, as he carried me. Within seconds, my back was on the soft couch, and his body hovered over mine. Sam gazed at me with so much affection that my heart ached. He touched my lips with his finger, and I lightly sucked on it, making him groan.

He kissed me again, trailing down to my neck and collarbone, while his hands deftly unbuttoned my pants. I was lost in the sensations he stirred in me, his lips at my ear distracting me so completely that I didn't even notice when his hand slipped into my underwear, gently stroking me. I let out a loud moan, and he smirked.

"Looks like we only get scandalous during sex, eh, Elena?"

"Maybe it's because we're just that good at it," I teased.

His proud smile faded as he kissed me again, his fingers working their magic. Just as I was about to climax, he pulled away, and I groaned in frustration.

"You're a bit overdressed for my taste," he teased, sliding my pants and underwear off, leaving me bare from the waist down.

Sam kissed his way back up, starting at my feet and working his way to my knees and thighs until he was settled between them. When I felt his mouth on me, I gripped his hair and held my breath. "For fuck's sake, Martin," I gasped.

I could feel his smile against my skin, and it only made me want him more. There was no better sight than Sam's head between my legs, making me feel things that seemed impossible even in God's eyes. His hands slid up my body, under my t-shirt, unhooking my bra and freeing my breasts. His fingers teased my nipples, pinching just right, while his tongue worked its magic. The combination of his touch and mouth sent me into an intense orgasm that made my entire body tremble.

When I came back down to Earth, he was lying beside me, a

satisfied grin on his face. "Miss me?" Sam asked, brushing his nose against mine.

"A little," I teased, before pushing him playfully. "But where's the rest, Martin? We've been apart for weeks. I'm not done yet."

He laughed, his eyes sparkling. "You'd better be ready for a whole weekend of wild sex, Elena. And for the record, I'm nowhere near finished."

I smiled and pushed him back onto the couch. "Good, because I didn't fake being sick at work and run off for nothing." I straddled his stomach, starting to unbutton his shirt.

"Nothing? You call this chaos you've caused in my living room nothing?" he mocked, pretending to be shocked.

I shrugged with a smile.

"It was a solid start," he defended, but I silenced him with a kiss.

He stayed quiet as I undressed him, watching me with those intense eyes. Every now and then, our gazes locked, and he'd give me a shy smile. I could see the desire in his eyes, the flush of his cheeks. I kissed and nibbled along his body as I removed his clothes, mirroring his own movements as if to show him how he made me feel. His body was different—more defined but still lean. So impossibly hot. My hands roamed over him, purposefully grazing his inner thighs just to see his reaction. I teased, acting like I was going to use my hands, and watched him tense up, completely turned on. But instead, I knelt in front of him and took him into my mouth.

"Fuck," he whispered. His head between my legs was my favourite sight, but his moans were my favourite sound. He threaded his fingers through my hair. "You're going to be the death of me," he said through gritted teeth, and I couldn't help but laugh.

"There are worse ways to go, Martin. Don't complain."

He bit his lower lip, which only urged me on. I took him all the way to my throat, and Sam clenched his fist. "Elena..." he practically sang my name.

When I knew he was close, I pulled away and looked up at him innocently.

"What the hell?" he groaned, staring at me, stunned.

"Where are the condoms in this place?" I asked, smiling like I hadn't just denied him an orgasm.

Frustrated, he sprinted to the kitchen island where his wallet was. He grabbed a condom and tossed it to me, making me laugh. Determined to keep driving him crazy, I put the condom on him using only my lips. Just as I was about to take control again, he flipped me onto the couch.

"You're dangerous when you're in charge," he chuckled. With a swift move, Sam pulled off my t-shirt and bra, removing the last barriers between us.

Before I could say anything, he entered me, making me gasp.

"You okay?" he asked, nibbling the corner of my mouth.

I just nodded, and he smiled.

Sam started slow, his movements deliberate, but that didn't last long. We were desperate for each other, craving that shared explosion of pleasure. At that moment, I wanted nothing more than to feel his muscles tense beneath my fingers as he moaned my name.

"Elena, I..." he began, but I covered his mouth with my hand.

"Some things don't need to be said, Martin."

We held each other's gaze for a few intense seconds, our breaths mingling. I knew if I didn't stop him, we'd both end up saying things that would change everything. When I felt his lips curve into a smile beneath my hand, I slid it down to the back of his neck, pulling him into a kiss. I couldn't hold out much longer and soon climaxed around him, moaning softly as he buried his face in the crook of my neck, letting his weight rest on me.

We stayed like that for a while, his head on my chest, my fingers threading through his hair. Neither of us spoke until his phone broke the silence. He sighed and got up, searching through our discarded clothes.

While Sam took the call, I slipped into my underwear and threw on his shirt before flopping back onto the couch.

"My bed's here," he said with a grin.

"Great. More furniture for us to break in."

He laughed, leaning down to give me a quick kiss. "You should probably wear something other than my shirt. The delivery guys are coming up, and it wouldn't be great for them to see you like this."

"Let them look," I teased, stretching out on the couch.

"Ha-ha, very funny." He tossed me my pants, and I started getting dressed. When I moved to take off his shirt and hand it back, he stopped me. "Keep it. I'll just put on my jacket. Want one? It's getting cold in here."

He glanced at the thermostat, frowning at it like it was broken.

"Sam," I called out. When he turned, I gestured to the open window.

He rolled his eyes, laughing as he went to close it. We'd been so caught up that we hadn't even noticed.

When the delivery guys showed up with the king-size bed, we were both dressed, and the apartment looked decent—no clothes scattered, cushions back in place.

After they left with a generous tip from Sam, we exchanged a look and ran to the bedroom, laughing like teenagers. We never seemed to get enough of each other.

CHAPTER NINE
Elena

LET'S BE HONEST FOR A SECOND: I'M NO CHEF. NOT even close. I can whip up a few dishes, but nothing that would ever land me on *MasterChef*, that's for sure. But when I tasted the grilled chicken with lemon cream and garlic I'd just made, I had to give myself a little credit. It was actually pretty good. I carefully plated the chicken and potatoes, adding a sprinkle of parsley on top. What a masterpiece!

Sam hadn't let me out of his sight all weekend—figuratively speaking, of course. After our third round of sex on Friday, we ordered lunch and headed to my place to grab some clothes and essentials. We decided his apartment felt too empty and split up for a shopping trip. I took on the task of stocking the pantry since he warned me that all he had were chocolate chip muffins and some other questionable choices. While I was at Whole Foods, he picked up more furniture from that store I'd visited at Eaton Centre. We met back at his place later that evening.

On Saturday morning, Sam went to his parents' house to get the rest of his stuff. He asked if I wanted to join him, but I declined.

Meeting the parents was a big step, and I wasn't quite ready for that level of closeness with the Martins.

As I replayed the weekend in my mind and admired my culinary efforts, I heard the gentle notes of a piano coming from the room Sam had turned into a mini studio. He'd chosen the smaller bedroom, right next to his own en suite, just off the living room.

I tiptoed over, trying not to make a sound. He usually got shy and stopped singing when he knew I was listening. But this time was different. Sam saw my reflection in the window and smiled. I leaned against the doorframe, crossing my arms, and sighed as his voice filled the room.

"The simplicity of the notes / fills my ears / It was like the sight of her in the back of my eyes / had been there for all these years."

His fingers glided effortlessly over the keys of his electric piano, as if it were the most natural thing in the world. Well, for him, it was. For the rest of us mere mortals, it was a bit more complicated. And though I was familiar with his incredible falsettos, Sam sang full notes this time, reaching such pure tones that I got goosebumps. His neighbours were so lucky to hear him sing like this, his angelic voice filling the air. I just hoped he knew how special he was.

"Each moment we make / and each song we sing," he continued, glancing at me through the window. *"Are memories I'll always play / Every laugh and every moment / all safe inside the melody / written deep in my heart for all time."*

Correction: his neighbours were lucky, but I was the luckiest. And maybe staying together after his tour wouldn't be so bad. We wouldn't have any more conflicts of interest, and it might actually work. Sam looked back at me and smiled. I walked over, leaning down to kiss the top of his head, my elbows resting on his shoulders. He took my hands and intertwined our fingers, playfully biting one of them.

"Life should be simpler," he murmured, leaning back against me.

"Agreed," I said, resting my chin on his head. We stayed like that, lost in our thoughts, for a few minutes. "Dinner's ready."

Sam glanced up at me, making a face. “I’m a little scared to find out what you’ve made.” He winced as I swatted his chest.

“Prepare to be amazed, Martin!” I teased, kissing him quickly before heading back to the kitchen, with Sam trailing right behind me.

Life pulled us out of our bubble that Monday. Sam didn’t ask me to stay, but I couldn’t bring myself to leave. Going back to his place after work just felt natural, so I didn’t think twice before heading there each night. It was the week of the Icon Records gala, and I had everything set—dress, shoes, accessories, even my appointment at the salon.

When my alarm went off on Wednesday, Sam was still sound asleep beside me, his head resting on my shoulder. His bed was massive, but neither of us could sleep without some part of us touching. I got up carefully, trying not to disturb him, and slipped into the en suite bathroom to shower. I took off his t-shirt, my new favourite sleepwear, and tossed it into the laundry basket. I grimaced when I noticed how full it was. We’d accumulated so much laundry that I made a mental note to remind Sam to deal with it later. I stepped into the shower, letting the hot water wash over me, relaxing me and pushing away any lingering thoughts.

After drying my hair with the blow dryer I’d brought over, I got dressed. I kissed his forehead, grabbed my phone from the bedside table, and headed to the kitchen. I was scrolling through emails, completely distracted, when I bumped into something—or rather, someone.

“Oh my God!” A woman’s voice exclaimed. My heart stopped when I looked up. “I’m so sorry, I didn’t realize my son had company.”

I must have gone as white as a sheet.

“Let’s start over, shall we? Hello, I’m Katherine.” She extended a hand with a friendly smile, her British accent catching me off guard. I forced myself to shake it, barely able to breathe. “I’m Sam’s mother. You must be Elena, right?”

I wanted the ground to swallow me whole. Why hadn’t he told me his mother had a key to his apartment? Better yet, why hadn’t he warned me she might show up unannounced? I just wanted to disappear, to escape from this humiliating situation as fast as possible.

Sam must have sensed something was off because he stumbled out of the bedroom, looking half-awake, his hair a mess as he rubbed his eyes. “Mom?” He sounded confused.

“Good morning, darling,” Katherine said, hugging him. “I’m sorry if I caused any awkwardness. I didn’t know you had a guest. I just thought I’d surprise you and make breakfast before work, but I ended up surprising Elena instead.”

“D-don’t worry, it’s fine,” I stammered, feeling my face flush with the heat of a thousand suns. I could barely look at her, the embarrassment overwhelming. “I was just leaving.”

I desperately wanted to vanish—out of that apartment, that building, the city, the country, the planet—anywhere but there. The level of mortification I felt was off the charts.

“Oh, don’t be silly.” She waved her hand dismissively. “I’ve been your age, you know. Just promise me you’re being safe and everything will be fine.”

“Mom!” Sam yelped, clearly mortified.

“I really need to go,” I said quickly, bolting for the door. Sam rushed over, holding my coat and boots. As I pulled them on, I pointed a finger at him. “We’re talking about this later.”

I threw my loafers at him, and when the elevator doors opened, I stepped in without looking back, too afraid to meet the eyes of the most unexpectedly charming person I’d ever met.

"What do you mean, your parents know about us?" I was stunned. Sam and I were having dinner at my place because I refused to go back to his.

"I told my dad, and he couldn't keep it from her," he said, shrugging. "It's no big deal, Lena. And my mom loved you!"

Right, of course. You find your son's girlfriend—who's ten years older than him—coming out of his bedroom, and it's no big deal. Yeah, right.

"For the love of God, Martin!" I groaned. "Please tell me you were at least the one who did the laundry. I'm begging you!"

He pressed his lips into a thin line, trying not to laugh, and I closed my eyes, taking a deep breath.

"Do you want me to lie or tell you the truth?" His voice was full of amusement, which only made things worse.

"Tell me a damn lie." I pushed my half-eaten dinner into the trash, my appetite gone.

"Yes, I did the laundry," he said, and I leaned against the kitchen counter, staring at the wall. I felt his hands slide up my arms and rest on my shoulders, giving me a much-needed massage. "Relax. My parents know there's a part of my life that's private, and they're okay with that. It won't happen again, I promise."

Sam kissed the back of my neck and gently turned me to face him.

"Come home with me," he whispered.

"I am home," I grumbled, still feeling annoyed.

He rolled his eyes. "Come to your second home, then. Or third, if you count your parents' place."

"I'm never setting foot in that apartment again, Martin," I vowed. "Never. God, your mom did my laundry!"

"Of course she did," he said, taking the dishes to the dishwasher. "Do you really think I know how to do laundry? I have no clue how that machine works."

I buried my face in my hands. "This is so embarrassing!"

I couldn't decide what was worse: bumping into Katherine—who probably heard me in the shower and drying my hair—or having her son deliver my freshly laundered clothes, which she had washed herself. I felt his arms wrap around me and couldn't help but laugh. When I looked up, he had a goofy grin, and I couldn't keep from laughing too.

"But she really did like you," he said proudly, and I rolled my eyes. "Oh, and I almost forgot. I have something for you. My mom dropped it off this morning."

"What?" Please don't let it be some family heirloom.

Sam went to the living room and came back holding a black velvet box. "Her best friend owns the jewellery store where I got it." He handed me the box, and I opened it, my eyes widening. "It's simple, like I promised. I hope you like it."

Inside was a pair of earrings that sparkled like they were made of stars. They were just two square 5-carat diamonds set in white gold. Elegant, understated, and they would look perfect with the sequins on my dress.

"Do you like them?" His voice sounded nervous.

I pulled him in by the neck, kissing him softly. "I love them! Thank you!" He let out a sigh of relief. "But I'm still not over bumping into your mom this morning!"

Sam laughed loudly and pulled me into a hug, lifting me off the kitchen floor and spinning me around, making me giggle like I hadn't in years.

I stared at the woman in the mirror, completely mesmerized. I smiled, and she smiled back, the black dress hugging her curves perfectly. My hair was styled in a loose updo, leaving my back exposed, and the diamond earrings shimmered as I checked my makeup. My eyes were dark and defined, balanced by a subtle nude lipstick. I had to admit it: I looked hot as hell.

My phone buzzed with messages. One was from Sam, asking to see my dress, but I declined. He'd just have to wait and see it in person. Another was from the driver hired by Icon Records, confirming he was outside. John's message said he was stuck in a meeting and would be a little late.

We'd agreed to meet at the party, and that was that. I slipped my phone and lipstick into my clutch and headed out, a mix of excitement and nerves bubbling inside me.

Fifteen minutes later, the driver pulled up in front of the Four Seasons, one of Toronto's most luxurious hotels. The decorations were stunning—white flowers, black tablecloths, and gold accents everywhere. It was miles ahead of last year's event. The hostess guided me to my team's table. Sam wouldn't be sitting with us, as the artists had their own section.

As I approached, I saw Vicky, Morgana, and Peter already seated.

"My. God. In. Heaven," Peter exclaimed. "Who are you, and what have you done with our Elena?"

I threw my head back, laughing. "Hey, once a year, we can work miracles, right?"

The table erupted in laughter. Soon, Matt and Katie joined us, and we were deep in conversation about the decor and everyone's outfits when Morgana sighed dreamily.

"Here he comes."

We all turned to see Sam entering the room, dressed in a classic black tuxedo. He looked like he'd stepped straight out of a fashion campaign, his hair artfully tousled. When he spotted me, his smile lit up the room, sending a swarm of butterflies fluttering in my stomach.

"Hello, everyone," he greeted, making his way around the table.

He hugged and shook hands, and just as he was about to reach me, a colleague caught my attention. I turned to chat briefly, and when I turned back to Sam, his surprised expression made me grin. He pulled me into a hug, holding me just long enough to whisper in my ear:

"What the hell is this? Are you trying to kill me?"

His hand lingered on my back for a moment, sending shivers through me. But too soon, his agent whisked him away to his own table.

About half an hour later, the person I'd been waiting for finally arrived. I could hardly believe he was here, even though he'd said he would be. When our eyes met, his face lit up with a huge smile, and I felt a sense of comfort wash over me.

"Lena," he murmured into my hair as we hugged.

"John!" My voice was filled with excitement. "I can't believe you're here! I've missed you so much!"

He kissed my forehead, and I leaned into his familiar warmth as his hand gently rubbed my back, the way only John knew how. It was like coming home. He spun me around, making sure I knew just how stunning he thought I looked.

John was ridiculously handsome—chiseled jaw, thick beard, and eyes that changed shades depending on the light. His hair was always perfectly styled, and his arms were covered in tattoos, my favourite being the lion surrounded by geometric shapes on his right arm.

He sat beside me, and we quickly fell into a conversation, picking up where we'd left off. John was my rock. We'd met at Icon Records years ago, on my first day. He was the only one who saw through the cracks in my marriage and had never hesitated to point it out, even when I didn't want to hear it. Despite the harsh words I'd thrown his way, he'd stuck by me. When I'd ended up in the hospital after trying to escape my ex, John was the first to show up. He was more than a friend; he was family.

After my divorce, he'd moved in for a few weeks until I felt safe on my own. We'd become so close that people thought we were more than friends, but that was never the case.

We sat facing each other, my legs resting between his, his hand comfortably on my thigh. We hadn't seen each other since he'd transferred to New York, a move Jeremy had never quite forgiven him for. But John was a talent magnet, and everyone wanted him on their team. It didn't take long for Jeremy to appear, pretending to be annoyed.

"If you're trying to steal Elena, give it up now," he grumbled. The two of them exchanged a quick handshake and hug.

John wrapped his arm around me, pulling me closer. "That's not your call, Jeremy. Elena will work with me someday, and we'll make the New York office the best in the world."

"She would never betray me like you did. Right, Elena? You're not moving to New York, are you?"

I laughed. "Right now, I'm not planning on it, Jer. But 'never' is a strong word."

Movement at the back of the room signalled the start of the evening's second show. Jeremy returned to his table as the lights dimmed. I glanced towards the stage, catching Sam's gaze. John followed my eyes and smirked.

"How's your puppet doing?" he teased. I rolled my eyes, but he continued, "Please, Lena. I can recognize when a star is being well fucked. He's head over heels."

"I don't know what you're talking about," I said, taking a big gulp of my champagne.

"Sure you don't." John tucked a loose strand of hair behind my ear. "Let's see if he can keep it together tonight."

I gaped at him. "Don't you dare!"

John just laughed, clearly enjoying himself. "I love a good game." He kissed the corner of my mouth just as the mic screeched.

"Good evening, ladies and gentlemen," Sam's voice boomed through the speakers.

John chuckled. "Quicker than I thought."

I didn't want to mess with Sam's head tonight. We hadn't had a chance to talk, and I hadn't introduced him to John as planned. I'd told him he'd love meeting my friend, and now he was up there watching as John nearly kissed me.

The girls at our table were buzzing, singing along to the first song Sam played. I knew his setlist by heart, so I wasn't surprised by his choices. But I couldn't shake the feeling that he was sending me messages through the lyrics, like he was speaking directly to me. Or maybe I was just overthinking it.

"Shall we dance?" John whispered in my ear, startling me. "Yes, I'm asking you to dance to your boy's song. Let's go!"

He didn't wait for my answer, pulling me onto the small dance floor in front of the stage. We'd danced together so many times before that I didn't have to think, just follow his lead. His hand was firm on my back, guiding me with ease.

"Elena, I don't want to freak you out," he said softly as we turned, giving me a clear view of Sam, "but I think the kid is in love with you."

I laughed, unable to take him seriously. John was great at reading people, but he also loved to stir the pot. The song ended, and we made our way back to the table, his hand resting on my lower back. As we sat down, I glanced over at Sam, who was now seated at the piano. He caught my eye, and I smiled, but he just turned away, starting to play Compassion.

He kept sneaking glances at me during the song, his gaze intense and full of something I couldn't quite decipher. John noticed too, and I could feel his tension rising.

"I am everything I have / that is why I'm asking for / a little compassion."

Sam's voice was raw, his eyes locked on mine, and John muttered a curse under his breath. Sam tried to play it cool, looking around the room, but it was obvious. He was singing to me, baring his soul in front of everyone.

"Take my heart, break me down to bits / I'll do anything you want, give you everything / I'm all yours, proudly and fearlessly."

"That's enough," John growled beside me. "Let's get out of here."

He was serious, protective, and I knew he was right. We couldn't afford to be reckless. So I followed him out of the party, holding his hand as Sam's voice pleaded for compassion. I didn't look back.

The gala had finally arrived. I couldn't wait to see Elena all dressed up. I tried to get her to send me a photo of her outfit, just to admire her for a bit, but she wouldn't budge. She was firm about keeping it a surprise. Tania, my stylist, suggested I wear something different, but I stuck with a classic look. I didn't want to risk not matching Elena's style.

During the drive to the Four Seasons, I scrolled through social media, hoping to catch a glimpse of her. But she wasn't the type to pose at the entrance for photos. She probably darted straight inside, avoiding the cameras.

When the car stopped, I got out, smiling at the flashes hitting me from all directions. Blinded by the lights, I made my way into the ballroom with Alex, my manager, by my side. My eyes swept across the room until I spotted her—stunning in a long black sequin dress. The front was modest, with a high neckline and long sleeves, just as I'd expected. Elena was reserved and discreet; she would never wear anything with a plunging neckline. Or at least, that's what I thought.

I approached her team and began greeting them one by one. Just as I was about to talk to her, a petite woman called her name. Elena turned around, and I lost my footing. Her dress, modest in the front, was completely open in the back, leaving her flawless skin on full display for others to see. The cut of the dress stopped just above her ass, and all I wanted was to tear her out of that damned outfit and devour her until morning. Elena looked so beautiful, sexy, and irresistible that I had to hold my breath when she turned back to me. Her wide smile was painted with a natural shade of lipstick, while her eyes were highlighted with mascara and other makeup I couldn't even begin to name.

When we hugged, her citrusy perfume hit me hard. I was one lucky bastard to have that woman in my life.

"What the hell is this?" I growled. "Are you trying to kill me?"

I knew she was. Elena wanted to see me at her feet, crawling for her. That had to be the reason she chose that dress. And even though I knew she was wearing it for herself, I couldn't help but dream it was for me. I could hardly wait to drag her to my room and have her all to myself.

Alex pulled me over to our table, and I quickly reached into my pocket, grabbing my phone to send Elena a message.

You look stunning. Definitely the most beautiful woman here.

She didn't reply. In fact, I hadn't seen her with her phone at all. And I knew she hadn't even glanced at it, because I hadn't taken my eyes off her. I was completely captivated by Elena and her sparkling dress. A stupid grin spread across my face when I noticed she was wearing the earrings I had given her. Yes, I was her date, even if from a distance.

After some time, a guy approached, and Elena stood up, hugging him with more affection than I would've liked. Her lips said his name with admiration: John. Damn it, he was the one who had invited my girl to accompany him to the party. He spun her around, taking in the sight of her. I noticed he complimented her, and Elena smiled sweetly. That smile should have been mine, not his.

I grabbed my phone again and sent another message. Maybe if her phone vibrated on the table, someone would let her know.

Aren't you going to introduce me to your friend?

Nothing. Elena was completely absorbed in him, not once taking her eyes off that perfectly chiseled face. I clenched my fists and locked my feet around the legs of my chair. I wanted to get up and pull him away from her. The guy was like a vulture, circling around her, not letting anyone else get close. Even when Jeremy came over to talk to her, he pulled her by the waist, pressing his body against hers. I gritted my teeth and looked away. The smile she was giving him was making me sick.

She had said I'd love to meet her friend. In that moment, I couldn't think of anyone I hated more than him. Who was this guy, anyway? What was so special about him? Sure, he was handsome, I couldn't deny that. But what did he have that made Elena so fixated on him, ignoring everyone else? Not even glancing at me?

I felt like a discarded toy, tossed aside when she found someone better to hang out with. Ugh, don't think like that, Martin. Don't let your mind go there, imagining Elena and John in bed. I sent another message.

Elena, can we talk?

But she still didn't reply. My girl had eyes only for that damned John, and she only stopped talking to him when someone interrupted them. Minutes later, the event organizer came to tell me my show was up next, and I stood up. My legs were shaking, but I knew going over there would only make things worse, so I headed straight to the stage. I was tuning my guitar when I noticed they were sitting very close. The bastard looked at me. With a smug grin, he said something to Elena, who scolded him. John didn't care and kissed the corner of her mouth. My blood boiled, and I fiddled with the microphone, making it screech. What I really wanted was to punch him right in the face and knock out all those perfectly straight, white teeth!

The show was a disaster. Every song annoyed me, and I was furious. Not even the gorgeous women showing off in front of the stage could distract me from Elena. When John led her to the dance floor and they started moving together, a painful lump formed in my throat. He glanced at me again, rubbing her back—the same back I loved kissing while she rested after we'd made love. The most beautiful back I'd ever seen, and it looked magnificent in that dress.

John twirled her around, and Elena didn't seem to care. This wasn't my stubborn girl who only did what she wanted. Did he put something in her drink?

The piano was placed in front of me, and I got ready to play. She finally looked at me and smiled, but I didn't smile back. My head was pounding, and all I wanted was to understand why. What had I done to deserve such humiliation?

Compassion was a beautiful song, one I loved, but right then, it felt like a plea to Elena. I just wanted her to stop stomping on my heart like that. We had been fine, spent days together, and even laughed over that incident with my mom. And now, my girl was in another man's arms, completely ignoring my feelings. It wasn't fair!

The song was almost over, and I sang as loudly as I could, pushing my lungs and vocal cords to their limits in a desperate attempt to make Elena stop. But John seemed irritated, whispering something to her, though she didn't respond. Well, she spoke with her eyes, eyes I couldn't see because they were fixed on his damn face.

Hand in hand with that guy, Elena quickly said goodbye to her team and walked towards the door, while I sat there at the piano, pleading for compassion. The last thing I saw was their exchanged glances before John wrapped his arm around her shoulders and they disappeared into the hallway, both smiling.

I sang the final song with great difficulty and rushed off the stage straight to the bathroom, where I vomited up my dinner and all the words I hadn't been able to say to Elena.

CHAPTER TEN

Sam

I HAD NO IDEA WHERE TO LOOK FOR ELENA ANYMORE. I'd been wandering around the hotel corridors for hours, pretending I was searching for my room even though I didn't have one. But I knew she was there with that goddamn John, and I had to find her. This urgency was pounding in my chest, driving me to figure out what the hell had happened, and why she'd done this to me. To *us*.

Even though I couldn't be sure she was still at the Four Seasons, I couldn't let myself believe she'd gone home. If she had, it meant John was with her, and I couldn't bear the thought of them lying in the bed where I'd loved Elena so many times. I'd have to burn the damn thing and buy a new one because I'd refuse to ever set foot on it again. I almost laughed at myself. She'd put on this whole show, letting that asshole have her all night, and here I was, still thinking about getting back in her bed. God, I needed help.

My feet were killing me, and I gave up. I slumped down at the end of a long corridor I'd paced back and forth a hundred times. I stared at the plastic cup in my hand, watching the ice melt into nothing. I groaned, frustrated. The alcohol was watered down now, and it wouldn't do much. Not that I needed it—I was already pretty hammered. One of the perks of being legal? You could drink as much as you wanted. The downside? You could drink too much, just like I had, and then suffer for it the next day. But right now, at 2 a.m., I couldn't care less. I needed something to get me through the night until I found her.

I pulled out my phone and tried calling her again, but it went straight to voicemail, just like the last sixteen times I'd tried. No, I wasn't counting—my phone was. I frowned as my thoughts scrambled for a moment, and I had to remind myself why I was even there. Oh, right. Elena.

A door clicked open down the hallway, and I glanced up, searching for where the sound came from. And there she was. My girl, stepping out of one of the rooms in the middle of the fucking night. Her hair was down now, falling over her shoulders. Her lips, no longer painted that light colour, were back to their natural shade, the one that always made me want to kiss her the second I saw them.

She didn't notice me, sitting there like a fool, humiliated, waiting for her to come out of *his* room and give me some kind of explanation. Elena walked to the elevator and pressed the button, turning her phone on as she waited. The soft ding echoed in the hallway, and she stepped inside, disappearing behind the closing doors, leaving me breathless and on the verge of tears, like the stupid kid I was.

Elena

John decided to stay with us for Christmas, and I was more than pleased about that, though a part of me felt empty. Sam wasn't responding to my messages or answering my calls, and I knew I deserved it. I just wanted a chance to explain.

My parents were thrilled when we arrived at their house. We were greeted with hugs, kisses, and my mom's M&M cookies fresh out of the oven. After everything that had happened and all the support John had given me, he'd become like the son they'd never had. They even set up a room for him at their place.

Going back to my parents' home always brought comfort. As an only child, I'd been spoiled, but they'd always listened and supported me, even when I made mistakes. My mom noticed something was off when I checked my phone for the third time in less than ten minutes. She called me into her room, and we talked for hours. I told her everything—how I met Sam, what our relationship was like, and where things stood now. She was upset at first, angry at what I'd let happen, and for what had gone down at the party. I could understand that. Even though John was like a brother to me, Sam didn't know that and must've been hurt.

"I never thought this would happen, Mom," I said through tears. "But I really care about him. Despite everything, I love him. And it's so hard to say that because I don't know if I've shown it. If I did, he wouldn't be so distant. I messed everything up!"

"Give the boy some time, Elena," she advised. "From what you've said, Sam has a busy few weeks ahead. He needs space to cool off so you two can talk. And stop stressing about the age difference. Did you forget I'm eight years older than your dad? It never stopped us from building a life together and having an incredible daughter."

I smiled softly and hugged her tight. I tried to give Sam space, but on Christmas evening, my hands betrayed me, and I ended up calling him.

"Elena," he answered. My heart stopped.

"Hi, Sam." My voice was shaky. "How are you?"

"Good."

God, this was going to be harder than I thought. "I... Merry Christmas." I sighed.

"Thank you. Merry Christmas to you too."

"I'm at my parents', and I don't think I'll be back before you leave for Jamaica again."

"That's okay, no worries."

Silence. I could hear him breathing on the other end.

"I'm sorry," I blurted out.

"Me too."

"Goodbye." And I hung up.

Tears streamed down my face as John walked into my room, freezing when he saw me crying. "What happened?" He rushed over and sat in front of me.

"He's never going to talk to me again, John." I sobbed like a child who'd just broken her favourite toy. "I've lost him forever."

"Lena." He sighed and pulled me into a bear hug. "It'll be okay. For now, it's best if you two stay apart. It was obvious at the party—he's in love with you. I could feel it from across the room. I know it's getting harder to hide, but you both need to wait for his tour to end. You'll be on another project, he'll have a different team, and no one will be able to say a thing."

"Am I an idiot for falling for someone so much younger?"

John chuckled. "Lena, I hadn't seen that big smile on your face in ages. If it's because of a guy who's barely out of diapers, then so be it. And you should accept that because there's clearly love in that little heart of yours." I pouted, and John wiped my tears away. "I know it's not an ideal situation, shorty, but your mom's right. Let's enjoy the holiday and eat everything we can, because neither of us can cook like she can. When Sam gets back from Jamaica, you'll talk, and it'll all work out."

"He hates you, John," I declared. "I'm sure of it."

He rolled his eyes. "I don't care, Elena. He doesn't need to like me—he needs to love you. He needs to respect you and encourage you to be the best version of yourself. And respect our friendship, obviously. If Sam Martin can do that, then I can listen to his music without gagging."

With the support of my parents and John, I managed to keep Sam out of my head for the most part until I got back to Toronto. He was supposed to fly in on Wednesday, and I was a ball of nerves. Why couldn't it be Wednesday already?

The first few days back were a nightmare. I kept rehearsing what I'd say in my head over and over. "Look, John is just a friend, and nothing happened after the party," I muttered to myself in the mirror.

God, maybe that wasn't the best approach. He'd probably ask what *did* happen, and I'd have to say I stayed in John's room until two in the morning talking about him. My friend had been so patient, even listening to our fights. I left out the more intimate details, but John knew more about Sam and me than anyone else.

On Monday and Tuesday, there wasn't much to do except obsess over the anticipation for Sam's new album. He was coming back to Toronto with everything recorded, and we just needed to finalize the marketing plan.

By the time Wednesday arrived, I thought my heart might explode. My parents and John sent encouraging messages, wishing me luck for the meeting. My friend even added, "and with him too," at the end, making me smile. The drive to Icon Records felt like it took forever, and I felt like I needed to pee every time someone said his name. We were already seated in the big meeting room when Martin finally showed up. I held my breath when our eyes met, and he smiled.

He. Smiled. At. Me.

That had to be a good sign, right? It seemed like Sam wasn't mad anymore, and my heart settled a bit. Everything would be okay. We'd talk, find a way to navigate through the rest of the tour, and then... well, then would be our story.

I was sitting in the middle of the rectangular table. Sam walked over to Jeremy, who was at the head, and handed him a small box. "It's all there," he said, smiling. "Hope you guys love it as much as I do."

When my boss placed the box aside, there were protests around the table.

"Aren't we going to listen to it?" Matt asked.

"No." Jeremy smirked, clearly enjoying the suspense. "I'll listen first, then share it with you. I want to see how much Elena has researched Martin's work and how well they align."

I sighed, disappointed. More than listening to the songs, I just wanted to hear Sam's voice. I wanted to jump across the table and hug him, kiss him, tell him I missed him.

The meeting didn't last long; we just reviewed the schedule. As we were leaving, Jeremy asked me to stay. For a moment, I considered lying and saying I had something urgent to work on. Sam was so close, but still so far, and we hadn't had a proper chance to talk. It was killing me.

As soon as everyone left, Marco, the lawyer, walked in with a stack of papers. Jeremy closed the door, a faint smile on his face.

"That was Sam Martin, wasn't it? The guy we met in Japan," Marco asked casually.

I swallowed hard.

"You met Martin in Japan?" Jeremy looked at me, puzzled.

"Yeah, we were having lunch when he walked in." Someone needed to shut this lawyer up. "He seemed surprised to see us, didn't he, Elena? I'd even say he panicked a bit when he saw you. I don't think he expected to bump into anyone he knew."

"Right, but what did you want to discuss, Jer?" I tried to steer the conversation away. I couldn't explain what Sam was doing in Japan without digging myself into a deeper hole. Marco set the papers on the table, and I noticed the bold letters at the top: *PROJECT TS*. A chill ran through me.

"This…"

"That's the contract for the marketing project with Taryn Steward," Jeremy said proudly, handing me a pen. I had to catch my breath. "If you're still interested, just sign here, and you're officially on her team."

With trembling hands, I signed it, barely believing I'd actually secured the project.

As I left the room, I was in a daze. I'd done it, and I was ecstatic. My smile grew even wider when I spotted Sam standing near my office door. He looked incredible—his skin lightly tanned, cheeks flushed from the Jamaican sun. A familiar heat ignited in my stomach. The desire was so intense, I wanted to pull him into my office right then and there.

When our eyes met, I could see he felt the same. The corner of his mouth lifted in a smirk, and I bit my lip. I glanced around, weighing my options. The corridor was empty, and there was only one possibility. I'd already taken risks for him before—why not again?

Just down the hall, there was a staff restroom. It wasn't as nice as the one for visitors, but it had a lock, and that's all I needed. His eyes followed mine, and he smiled knowingly.

I walked past him, heading straight for the restroom, not bothering to check if he was behind me. I knew he was. I stood in the middle of the small space, my heart pounding. The anticipation was both exhilarating and maddening. The wait was agonizing and thrilling at the same time—agonizing because I felt like I might combust any second, and thrilling because I knew he would make it worth every second.

When I heard the lock click, I grinned.

Sam's hands were gentle but firm as he turned me around to face him. I stared at his chest, taking in the black shirt that clung to his frame. His fingers brushed my jaw, tilting my head up. His pupils were blown, and when our lips finally met, it felt like my whole world exploded.

The intensity between us was overwhelming, an undeniable force that pulled us together. I couldn't fully comprehend my feelings for him; I loved him so much it ached. It was the kind of pain that gripped my soul, a relentless burn that spread wherever he touched me. It was a madness I'd never experienced in all my twenty-eight years of life.

Nothing compared to what we'd shared over these past months.

Sam groaned, and I clung to him, my nails digging into his neck. He drove me insane—always. Crazy in love, crazy with anger, crazy with anxiety, just completely crazy. And I trusted him so deeply that I didn't even hesitate to have sex in the company restroom because I knew he'd protect me from anything.

"God, Elena," he murmured, unbuttoning my pants. "I've missed you so much."

"I know," I replied, and he smiled.

In one swift motion, Sam stripped me of my clothes, leaving me half-naked. "We have to be quick, Lena, but I promise I'll make it up to you later." Promises. We usually avoided them, but I definitely wanted him to keep that one.

He lifted me onto the sink counter, positioning himself between my legs. I hurriedly unbuttoned his shirt and tossed it aside as he fumbled with his pants. I wanted to kiss him, undress him, admire him, and have him inside me—all at once. And when he finally entered me, I bit down on his shoulder to muffle my moan.

It felt so right, it was almost wrong. We were made for each other, and I was convinced of that since the day we met at that coffee shop. Sam's fingers dug into my waist as he moved, his rhythm urgent. The sensation of skin against skin was electrifying.

It didn't take long before I was falling apart in his arms, and he kissed me deeply, his voice breaking as he called my name.

"You're getting bolder," he teased, his voice breathless. "First, skipping work, and now pulling me into a restroom for a quickie."

"All your fault," I laughed, resting my head against his chest. "You give me those puppy-dog eyes, and I can't resist."

"You're trouble," he murmured, biting my cheek lightly before pulling me into a tight embrace. I closed my eyes, content to just stay there, wrapped in his warmth.

"We need to talk."

Sam kissed the top of my head. "I know. Come over to my place when you're done here."

I pouted. "Your mom won't be there, right?" I asked, feeling silly, and he chuckled.

"No, Elena. After that day, she always asks before dropping by. I think you might have traumatized her."

I looked into his eyes, and he held my face gently between his hands.

"Can I wait for you?"

"Always," I whispered, pulling him in for another kiss.

We got dressed and left separately, taking different routes back to the office. I was floating on cloud nine. I'd just completed an incredible project, signed on for an even bigger one, and reconnected with Sam. Things couldn't get any better. Well, maybe if I won the lottery and only worked for fun, donating all my earnings to charity, that would top it.

But I hadn't been in my office for long before Jeremy summoned me urgently.

"What's up, Jer?" I asked as I walked in, shutting the door behind me. He looked agitated, his expression tense.

"Elena, I'm going to be blunt because there's no way around this. Is there something going on between you and Sam Martin?"

I blinked, trying to process his question. "What do you mean?" I needed time to think. Did someone see us coming out of the restroom? That was impossible; the hallway was empty.

"You know exactly what I mean, Elena," he snapped.

"There's nothing going on between us."

Not good. My heart raced.

"Elena, for God's sake, tell me what's happening!" Jeremy insisted.

Since I stayed silent, Jeremy slid a sheet of paper across the desk. I picked it up, confused. Written in his awful handwriting were numbered lines, quotes that made no sense.

"What is this?"

"These are lyrics from Sam's latest songs," Jeremy explained, gesturing for me to sit. He hit play on his computer, and the opening notes of a track filled the room. "Track number two, *Anxious.*"

My stomach dropped as Sam's voice started singing lines he'd once sung to me in my living room. I felt a cold shiver run down my spine. He couldn't have...

"Martin mentioned meeting you at a coffee shop when we first spoke. Then on track nine, *It Was For You,* he sings about seeing you with someone else but thinking you looked unhappy. There's no mistaking how irritated he was by you and John at that party." Jeremy's words cut like a knife. "What was that, Elena? He was practically performing for you. And when you left, he bolted out like he'd been shot."

"Jeremy, this is ridiculous," I said, tossing the paper back on the desk. "I didn't know he had some kind of infatuation with me—"

"Elena," Jeremy interrupted sharply. "He followed you to Japan."

"He didn't go to Japan because of me!" I snapped, raising my voice.

"Are you sure?" Jeremy clicked on another track. "Track three, *You in Japan.* He sings about it being more than friendship. Then Marco mentions seeing him there, and Rento claims a man kicked him out of your room. Who was that, Elena?"

"Rento shouldn't be talking. He barged into my room, completely drunk, and was lucky to get out alive."

Jeremy leaned over the desk, his face inches from mine. "Who was in your room, Elena?"

"That's none of your business."

"When Sam Martin goes to Japan and spends the night in your hotel room—paid for by this company—yes, it is my business."

I didn't know what hurt more—Jeremy's words or Sam's betrayal. I had begged him so many times not to write about us, knowing it would cause problems. Now, I watched my career crumble over a few stupid lyrics. How could he do this to me?

"I'm going to ask you one last time, Elena." Jeremy's voice was steely, his trust in me shattered. "What's going on between you and Sam Martin?"

There was no point in lying anymore. Marco knew Sam had been in Japan, Rento knew there was a man in my room, and the lyrics were practically a confession. I shut my eyes, trying to find the right words. Nothing came out. "I'm sorry, Jeremy," I whispered.

"*Sorry?*" he shouted. "Elena, what the hell is this? You just signed the biggest contract of your career with this company, you're given opportunities people would kill for, and you're telling me you're sorry for sleeping with a nineteen-year-old? Are you out of your mind?"

I had nothing else to say. I knew I'd messed up. I'd berated myself so many times for getting involved with Sam. Now it was too late.

"What am I supposed to tell the board?"

"They can't prove it, Jer."

"They don't need proof, Elena. They've got witnesses, and they've got a competitor for Martin who's more than happy to use this against you." His face turned red as he paced around the office, exasperated. "Did you stop to think, even for a second, about the chaos you'd cause if Rento decided to accuse you of violating the contract? You turned down the Japanese project because you were 'too busy' with the SM Project. And now I find out you weren't just working on the project, but the *artist* too. They could sue us!"

My vision blurred, and I felt the room spinning. I took a few deep breaths to keep from passing out. I knew all of this. What I didn't know was why Sam had decided to throw me under the bus like this. It couldn't have been because of John. He'd been doing this for a while, and I couldn't figure out why.

Jeremy ran his hands through his hair. "You could be fired, Elena," he said, and I let out a shaky breath. "And you probably will be."

Tears welled up in my eyes, a sharp pain stabbing at my heart. Icon Records was everything to me. My friends were here, my happiest memories. And now, they were going to kick me out because of Martin.

"Unless you can give me a damn good reason not to fire you. Did he force you? Is he blackmailing you?"

I shook my head. "Nothing I say can change what happened."

Jeremy stared at me for what felt like an eternity before dropping into his chair again. "You've screwed up everything, Elena. Your job, your career… all of it."

"Does the board know?" My voice cracked as I asked.

He nodded. "When I was listening to the song, Marco walked in with one of the directors." Shit. "He started talking about seeing you two in Japan, how Sam freaked out when he saw you. The man heard 'You in Japan' and put two and two together. He demanded answers, and I told him I didn't know what was going on. He told me to find out and report to legal."

I closed my eyes. This was a nightmare. "And now?"

"And now one of you—if not both—is getting dropped from Icon Records." If he'd slapped me, it would have hurt less.

"There has to be another way, Jer. This company is my life."

"Yeah, and you've messed with your life. You're under investigation, Elena. Can you believe that? One of our best leaders, now with a noose around her neck because of a nineteen-year-old kid!"

This was too much. I wasn't going down alone, and I wasn't going to lose everything because of him. It didn't matter how much I cared about Sam, he didn't get to walk away from this. I sprang up from the chair and snatched the paper off Jeremy's desk.

"Where are you going?" he yelled as I stormed out of the office.

I barely had time to grab my purse. It was freezing outside, but I was burning with anger, frustration, and hurt. Tears streamed down my face before I even realized I was crying. Everything he had touched seemed to burn, but not in the way I used to crave. Now, I wanted to tear my skin off, erase every trace of Sam Martin's scent, his touch, his kisses.

I called a taxi and gave the driver his address. Less than twenty minutes later, I was stomping through the lobby of his building, ignoring the receptionists who knew me all too well.

The elevator dinged on the eleventh floor, and I marched straight to his door. I didn't knock—I *pounded.* Screw the polite neighbours, or the fact that we, as Canadians, were supposed to be quiet and courteous. I wanted to break down that door, tear apart the entire building. After a few more punches, he finally opened it, looking terrified.

"Elena?" His face was a mix of shock and confusion. "What's wrong? Are you okay?" He reached for me, but I stepped back. I couldn't stand his touch right now. Just looking into his eyes was hard enough.

"What did you do, Sam?" I whispered.

I was trembling in the hallway, clutching that crumpled piece of paper in my hand. Martin looked at me, bewildered, not knowing what to do. He stepped aside, gesturing for me to come in. I only made it as far as the kitchen island.

"What are you talking about?" he asked.

I threw the paper onto the counter and watched as his eyebrows furrowed in confusion.

"*This*, Martin," I snapped. "This is what I'm talking about."

He picked it up and started reading, glancing at me every few seconds. I was falling apart—physically, emotionally, completely.

"How could you do this to me?" I sobbed, tears pouring down my face again. "How could you ruin my life like this?"

"Elena..."

"You did everything I begged you not to do. You made me the centre of attention, you exposed me to everyone!"

"There's no way they know the songs are about us!" He tried to reach for me, to calm me down, but I shoved his hands away. The anger I felt for him was suffocating, and I could barely breathe between words.

"They all know, Martin," I shouted. "Everyone! Jeremy found out, then Marco, even Rento knows. How could you be so stupid? How could you think you could talk about seeing me at a café and no one would connect the dots when they heard it in a song?"

I was screaming, louder than I thought I could. Let the neighbours hear me.

"Deny it; they have no proof." His voice was strained, and I could see he was losing his composure. "Elena, we can fix this. I'm sorry, I just thought..."

"Thought what?" I spat, the disgust clear on my face. "That I wanted some crappy songs about me out there?"

He took a step back. I hadn't meant to say that, but my adrenaline was spiking. I could feel electricity buzzing through my veins, my throat burning, and all I wanted to do was scream more.

"How are you going to deny it when Marco *saw* you in Japan, Sam? He *saw* you there, you two talked. And what did you do? You wrote a goddamn song about it!" I stepped closer, jabbing my finger at him. "It's over. My life is over, and it's your fault!"

I turned away, hiding my face in my hands as I cried. I was overwhelmed by a mix of anger and betrayal. I had trusted him, believed he'd protect me.

"I'll talk to Jeremy," he said desperately. "It'll be okay."

"One of Icon Records' directors found out, kid." I turned to face him, my eyes blazing. "They cornered my boss. I'm screwed. Can you even comprehend that? Your selfishness, your childish behaviour, and your complete lack of respect for me have put a noose around my neck. I'm getting fired, Martin."

"No," he gasped, stepping towards me, but I backed away again. "They have no proof, Lena. I'll just say they're just dumb songs, okay? Please, listen to me."

"They have *witnesses*!" I shouted back. "That asshole Rento told them there was a man in my room, and Marco confirmed you were there. They can even track our recent flights, Sam! Stop pretending you're still a teenager and grow the hell up! There are consequences to face, and I have the most to lose." We locked eyes, pain clear in both of us. "I signed a huge contract today, a once-in-a-lifetime opportunity. And you destroyed it all!"

"Elena, please, stop."

"I hope you're happy. You got what you wanted—you ruined me, Martin. And right now, I can't even tell you how much I *hate* you!"

He opened his mouth to respond, but his phone rang. I raised my eyebrows in warning, daring him to answer. If I meant anything to Sam, he'd focus on me and try to help, or at least listen to me while I raged in his kitchen. But he turned his back and took the call. He didn't care about my feelings or what I was about to lose. He didn't love me like I loved him.

I ripped off the earrings he'd given me and set them on the kitchen island. I walked out, the door slamming behind me just as I heard Sam shout my name. The elevator was still on the same floor, so I stepped inside, leaving for good.

I walked further than I should have without a coat. Eventually, I found a park some distance from his building and sat on a bench, crying like a child. I'd never truly been happy; that was the truth. I escaped an abusive husband only to end up with a reckless idiot who ruined my life and career. And the worst part was he didn't even understand what it meant to me. Sam was selfish, always focused on his own success, never caring about mine.

He'd never asked about my work or how I felt at Icon Records. He had nothing to lose—he was famous online, and any label would overlook an indiscretion to sign him. But me? When they reached out to Icon for a reference, they'd know what I'd done, and that would be the end.

My career in music marketing was over.

My phone rang constantly during the forty minutes I spent at the park. Sam was desperately trying to reach me, but there was nothing left to say. I couldn't even think about him. I felt betrayed, humiliated, and tired of always being the one who suffered.

The feeling of losing control of my life, of having no say in my own decisions, crashed back like a tidal wave, just like when I was with Noah. People thought they could make choices for me, leaving me voiceless. It was so absurd and infuriating, I laughed bitterly.

When my phone buzzed again, Jeremy's name lit up the screen. "I need you to come to the office, Lena," he said, his voice calmer than before. "We need to have an official conversation."

I got up from the bench and hailed a taxi. On the way, I wiped my face and tried to pull myself together. I didn't even realize how cold I'd been until I felt the warmth of the cab.

I headed straight to Jeremy's office, but he led me to a meeting room through a side door.

"John is on his way," he informed me, and I stared at him, stunned. "Yes, I called him. I never thought I'd say this, but I need that traitorous bastard right now. He should be here in three hours if he catches the next flight." I nodded. "You look wrecked."

"Thanks, I guess." I exhaled deeply.

Jeremy sat in front of me, and for the first time, I saw something beyond his usual pride—compassion and even a hint of regret.

"I'm sorry if I was harsh before, but I was furious, Elena. You've always been my best leader, and I didn't expect you to make such a serious mistake. I understand you have a private life, and if you and Martin are involved, that's your business." His tone was firm and serious. "But you should've stepped away from the project as soon as it started. Now I'm losing you, and I don't know what to do."

"Am I really getting fired?" I shut my eyes, bracing for the answer.

"I'll fight it, but I need your help, Elena. There's not enough space for both of you here anymore. If you stay, he goes. If he stays, you go. And I need the truth. If you declare you're innocent, I'll believe you and kick his ass out of here." His phone dinged with a message. "Martin's here," he said, and I jumped out of my seat.

"You called him?"

"Yes, but it's okay if you don't want to see him." Jeremy headed for the door. "I'll talk to him in my office. Stay here, and we'll talk to you after, all right?"

I nodded and sat back down, my leg bouncing with anxiety. My boss didn't close the door completely, and I could hear everything happening in his office. Sam and Alex entered, and I heard them sit in front of Jeremy's desk. Sam cleared his throat, anxious to get things moving.

"Martin, you know what's happening, and I hope you understand the gravity of your actions."

Sam stayed silent, shifting uncomfortably in his chair.

"My question is simple. Once I have your answer and Elena's, the board will decide your fate."

"Jeremy, it's not that serious," Alex interjected. "They're young; it happens."

"Other clients were involved, Alex. It *is* serious."

"So, what's the question?" Sam sounded tense.

"Who's responsible for all of this? Who initiated it?"

Jeremy's stern voice made me shrink in my seat. I closed my eyes, whispering a plea.

Please, just tell the truth, Sam. Just tell the fucking truth.

And then he spoke words I'll never forget.

"It wasn't me."

CHAPTER ELEVEN
Elena

IT WASN'T ME.

It wasn't me.

It wasn't me.

His words kept echoing in my head. I stared at the door, eyes wide and mouth slightly open, struggling to process what I'd just heard. My head throbbed, my stomach churned, but I was too stunned to even move. He'd blamed me. After everything that had happened, after chasing me, he had the nerve to say it wasn't him who started this. It was my fault.

Fortunately, Jeremy didn't believe him. "Sam, this is serious," he insisted. "Not only can Elena get fired, but she *will* be fired. So, I'm going to ask you one last time—who initiated this?"

"I've told you, man, it wasn't me."

My boss exhaled, clearly exasperated. I wanted to react, to express the same frustration, but I felt hollow, like all the air had been sucked out of me. It wasn't anger that filled me, just a heavy, crushing disappointment. A voice inside my head was screaming, *You knew this would happen,* and I couldn't make it stop.

I don't know how long I sat there, lost in thought. The sound of the office door slamming jolted me back to reality. Jeremy stormed into the meeting room, his face flushed, looking like he was ready to explode.

"You!" he roared, pointing at me. "You tell me the truth right now, because I can't wait to kick that little shit out of this company! He's not going to lie to my face, get you fired, and walk away like he's untouchable!"

And I knew he was right. I should have told Jeremy that Sam had shown up at my place after following me from Whole Foods, or that he'd flown to Japan against my wishes. But I was so exhausted—exhausted from being angry, scared, and on edge—that I did the one thing Jeremy wasn't expecting: I chose Sam.

"He's right, Jer," I said quietly. "It wasn't him."

My boss looked at me like I'd lost my mind. "Elena, don't start with this bullshit now. I know he's guilty—he practically admitted it to me. Even his agent looked shocked. Do you think I'm buying his story?"

"It was my fault, and I'm ready to face whatever comes. Call whoever you need to. I'll give them my statement, and I'll sign my termination papers."

"I'm not doing that!" Jeremy shouted. "You're going to tell them the truth, and we'll tear up his contract."

All I wanted to do was leave, go home, and never come back. I could find a quiet job in Dorchester, live near my parents, and get a pet. Life would be simpler, with far fewer things to worry about. Maybe that's what I needed. I'd refused to leave Toronto when everything fell apart with Noah, even though my parents begged me to move back. I thought staying here was my fate, that I couldn't abandon my career. But right now, I wanted to disappear. And let's be honest, as long as I stayed in the industry, I'd never truly get away from Sam. He'd sign with another label, and we'd keep crossing paths at award shows and events. I didn't want to spend the rest of my life hiding in bathrooms or watching him from backstage. Stepping away from music marketing didn't sound so bad after all.

"That's the truth, Jer," I insisted. "There's nothing more to say."

He stormed out of the room, muttering things I couldn't even make out. I knew he was furious, and I could only hope he and Sam wouldn't cross paths anytime soon. If they did, I had no doubt my boss would wring his neck. Meanwhile, I sat there, staring blankly at the white walls, my phone vibrating relentlessly with Sam's name flashing on the screen. I just wished he'd stop.

John was crouched in front of me, waiting for me to repeat the words he wanted me to say. But I just shook my head. He knew everything about how this had all started, but his word alone couldn't be used against Sam. Only I could make the final call, and I refused to change my story.

He stood up and asked Jeremy to leave the room. I stayed put, sitting in the same chair, in the same position, like I was too sick to move. I just existed, hoping something miraculous would happen. And as desperate as it seemed, I wanted Sam to walk in and tell the truth. But he never did.

I lost track of time, only realizing how late it was when I noticed the sun setting. Darkness had already taken over inside me, so it didn't feel much different. The guys came back, still caught up in their conversation.

"We're not making any decisions today, Elena," Jeremy said first. "Go home, get some rest. If you change your mind, come back tomorrow and tell us exactly what happened."

"I already told you what happened," I snapped, feeling my frustration boiling over. Why couldn't they just accept my confession and end this?

"Bullshit." He threw his hands up in the air. "You can repeat that nonsense a million times, and I still won't believe it. I know you, Elena, and I can't figure out why you're defending that stupid kid!"

John's expression was the angriest I'd ever seen. He reached out his hand, and I took it, getting to my feet and leaving the room with him.

"I'll take you home," he offered.

"No!" I stopped abruptly, and he turned to me. "Don't take me home. He'll show up, and I can't deal with him right now. Not tonight."

John raised his eyebrows. "Really?" he asked, his voice laced with sarcasm. "If you don't want to talk to him, why are you defending that little shit?"

I closed my eyes and took a deep breath.

"Goddammit, Elena! You're impossible." He took a breath, trying to calm himself. "Fine, you're coming to the hotel with me, and we'll figure things out tomorrow. And pray I don't run into him, because dead will be the nicest state he'll be in!"

I thanked John for always having my back, and we left. Once again, he was there to help pick up the pieces of me that were shattered all over the floor. And as if that wasn't enough, he didn't leave the next day or the day after. He stayed in Toronto, helping me manage everything while still sharing his hotel room with me. He even went to my house to grab my things so I wouldn't risk running into Sam.

Jeremy called him on Friday morning and asked us to come to Icon Records. John said he sounded both frustrated and relieved. We finished our breakfast and headed over.

"I'm trying to figure out what he wants," I said, eyeing John suspiciously as we sat in the back of the taxi. I saw his mouth tighten into a thin line. "You know, don't you?"

He shrugged. "I have a hunch, but I'm not going to say anything until I'm sure."

I rolled my eyes. When we arrived at the building, I found myself checking the area for any unwanted faces. John waited patiently, and when we got out, we headed straight to Jeremy's office.

"Finally!" my boss exclaimed. "Have a seat."

We did, and Jeremy settled into his chair, looking almost smug. There was some unspoken exchange between him and John that I couldn't decipher.

"Elena, if you still want to work at Icon Records, we have an offer for you."

"What?" I held my breath.

"You can still be with us, just not here in Toronto." Jeremy sighed. "Like I said, either you or Martin leaves. And since you won't be honest with us, we don't have much choice. You'll go, but to another branch."

My eyebrows shot up. "I don't understand."

"You're coming to New York with me," John said, barely able to contain his excitement.

"You jerk. I wanted to break the news!" Jeremy's laughter filled the room.

I glanced between the two of them, completely lost. How could they transfer me instead of firing me? Sam and I would still be at the same company. Wasn't that against some policy?

"Look," Jeremy continued. "The board can't afford to lose you, but they also can't break Martin's contract without your cooperation, and you won't give them that satisfaction. So, after some meetings and favours, we found a spot for you in our New York branch. You'll be working on Project TS, which will benefit from your direct involvement. It's a great opportunity."

This was the last thing I expected.

"Lena," John said gently. "We know you never planned on moving to New York, but this is the best option right now. Once this project wraps up, we'll talk to the board here and look at transferring you back. But for now, it's our only way out."

"Guys, this..." I was speechless. "Thank you. This is so much more than I expected. I know you're both taking risks standing by me, and I'm so grateful! I'll take this chance and move to New York, even though I love working here in Toronto. I promise you won't regret it."

"There are just two things you need to do first, Elena. First, take the fifteen vacation days you have left. You need it. As a friend, I'd suggest going to your parents' place to get some distance. You need a break, and it's best to get out of Toronto for a bit."

He was right. Gossip was probably spreading like wildfire, and staying here would only make things worse. Jeremy cleared his throat and exchanged a look with John. My friend sighed deeply.

"Are you serious?" The annoyance in his voice made me nervous.

"What?" I asked.

"Martin's putting on a secret show after his album release and before the tour. The decision was made yesterday. The entire team, along with fans and the media, will be there. And I'm sorry, Lena, but you can't skip it."

My jaw dropped.

"This is insane, come on," John muttered.

"I know this is a mess," Jeremy admitted, "but can you imagine how it would look if she didn't show up? Elena put everything into this project, and it would seem strange for her not to be there. Especially since everyone from Icon Records, including her team, will be present."

Hearing about my team made my heart sink. I'd miss them so much. We'd worked together for so long, and we had this unspoken bond—I could read their thoughts, and they could read mine. Just another thing Martin had taken from me.

I sighed and agreed. What couldn't be helped had to be endured, and there was nothing I could do to change things. Jeremy was right: going to my parents' was the best choice. Their love and support would help me deal with all the changes coming my way.

John handled my transfer to New York, staying in Toronto to sort out the logistics and help me pack up my house. Since I wasn't sure if

I'd ever return, I decided to sell it. Project TS would take at least two years, and I had no idea what New York held for me. I could rent, but I preferred to own a place in the U.S., and selling my home here was the best way to make that happen.

Sam's third album was about to drop, and I would return to Toronto for that damned concert. Before that, I'd stop by Icon Records to sign my transfer papers, then I'd watch his performance and fly to New York the next day. The timing was perfect—it would keep me busy and help me avoid Martin, even in my thoughts. His texts and calls were relentless, but I ignored them until I finally blocked his number. The last thing I needed was his pathetic excuses. He'd already done enough damage, and I never wanted to see that boy again.

Over the weekend, John brought some documents to Dorchester. My house sold faster than expected, and I was officially homeless in Toronto. My belongings would be on their way to New York in a few days, and the reality of it all started to hit me.

"There's a great apartment in my building," John said as we sat around the table, enjoying the pudding my mom had made for dessert. "Two bedrooms, lots of space, great layout. I think you could get a good price on it. I know the owner and can put in a word if you're interested."

"That would be wonderful, dear," my dad chimed in, his mouth full. My mom shot him a disapproving look, and we all laughed. "It would be good to have John nearby; he knows the area and the building. You should think about it."

And I did. John gave me the owner's number, and we chatted for a bit. The guy sent me pictures of the place and even offered a discount since the original price was a bit over my budget. Just like that, I signed the deal. I know buying an apartment without seeing it first is risky, but I trusted John. If he said it was a good place, that was enough for me.

Sadly, my vacation ended way too soon, and once again, I left my tearful parents behind. Growing up is tough in ways no one ever tells you. Everyone warns you about bills and responsibilities, but no one mentions how painful it is to watch your parents grow smaller in the rearview mirror.

When I saw the CN Tower appear from the bus window, my heart raced. We were so close to Sam's building that I closed the curtain, as if he could see me. Not that he would, but I wasn't taking any chances. John accompanied me to Icon Records, and when I got there, I couldn't believe my eyes. My team was throwing me a farewell party, and I couldn't hold back the tears. To quash any rumours, Jeremy told everyone I was invited to work at the New York office on one of the most important projects of 2019. He made sure everyone knew the board was thrilled to see one of their own being recognized, and I became the centre of attention—for a good reason, for once. When Jeremy handed me the papers to sign, Morgana and Katie started to cry. Minutes later, we were all hugging, sniffling, and already missing our time together.

"God, this is hard," I said in the elevator. John and Jeremy stood beside me, just like in the old days when I was an intern, and we were a tight-knit trio.

"Just promise you'll give it your all, Elena," Jeremy said, trying to hold back his emotions.

"I promise. And thank you, for everything, Jer. You saved me, and I'll never forget that."

We shared a quick hug in the lobby before I walked out, fighting back more tears. John draped his arm over my shoulders, pulling me close. He kissed the top of my head, and I wrapped my arm around his waist. "I can't believe I finally got you to come with me, shorty," he said, his joy palpable.

"Me neither," I replied, looking up at him. We shared a smile and headed to the hotel.

The only thing that soured the day, aside from leaving, was knowing I had to see Sam that night. Of all the things I'd dealt with these past few weeks, that was going to be the hardest. Jeremy was right: after all the sacrifices I'd made for this project, vanishing would raise suspicion, and I couldn't afford that. But, God, it was going to be brutal. Seeing that stage, facing the giant rose Matt and I had spent hours perfecting—it all brought back too many memories. I was just praying to get through the concert without falling apart.

John and I arrived just in time, minutes before the show started. I didn't want to have any chance of running into Sam backstage, of smelling his cologne or hearing him say my name. My heart had already taken enough hits.

As we made our way to the seats with the Icon team, something caught me off guard. Katherine, Miguel, and Amelia were there, sitting in the front row, waiting for their pride and joy to take the stage. When our eyes met, Sam's mom stood up, and I held my breath. She walked over to me, wearing an understanding smile, and pulled me into a tight hug. I closed my eyes and hugged her back, knowing this would be the only goodbye I'd get to say to him. She kissed my cheek gently and returned to her seat beside Miguel, who nodded at me with a polite smile before turning back to face the stage.

"Who are they?" John asked as I sat beside him.

"His mom, dad, and sister," I said, grateful he was the only one who seemed to notice what had just happened.

The lights dimmed, and the first notes of "You in Japan" played. The crowd went wild, screaming at the top of their lungs. I was struggling not to faint, but hearing the words he'd once used against me stung like hell.

At some point, our eyes met, and Sam's smile faltered when he saw John beside me.

"Bastard," John muttered, and I squeezed his hand.

All I felt was rage. I was starting to get used to the idea of moving to New York, but things could've been so different if Sam had just listened to me. But no, his ego couldn't handle that.

"Thank you, everyone," Sam said into the mic. "Before the next song, I want to give a shoutout to everyone who worked so hard to make this album and concert happen. Especially the team at Icon Records who worked tirelessly with me to bring you the best songs and experience possible. Toronto, let's give it up for this incredible team up there!"

He pointed at us, and the crowd erupted. My heart pounded so hard I thought it would burst. My hands were shaking as I forced a smile for my team and took a deep breath. He set his guitar aside and moved to the piano, playing a melody I didn't recognize. Maybe I would've, if I hadn't been avoiding his new album like the plague.

"I didn't believe it, so I needed proof / Just one touch of your lips, and I knew it was true." His voice was calm, his fingers gliding over the keys. *"It was poison / And I drank the best of it all."*

I felt eyes burning into me, but I kept looking at him, determined not to break as he continued.

"You sealed our fate / then set it ablaze." Our eyes locked, and my heart raced in my chest. John exhaled sharply beside me, shifting in his seat. *"But it was written in the stars / life was the death that tore us apart."*

From the corner of my eye, I saw Katherine turn to me, but I couldn't look at her. She knew the song was about me, just like the rest of the album. In any other situation, I might've felt flattered to be Sam's muse, but not now.

"We made a mess / But I can't stand to see you go." He found my eyes again. *"You're my whole world / So perfectly wrong for me."*

"That's enough," I muttered, standing up. John followed immediately. Sam wasn't going to use me as his personal therapy session anymore; he wasn't going to put my second chance in jeopardy.

Without looking back, I walked out, swearing to myself that Sam Martin would never crush my heart again, even if I had to tear it out of my chest myself. And I'd do it with my bare hands.

My plan had been perfect and straightforward. If I told Jeremy that Elena had seduced me, he would fire her, and I'd still have my contract. I was making good money and could support us both comfortably for as long as needed. In the meantime, Elena could start her own marketing company, if she wanted, and keep doing her brilliant work. I'd even encourage her to bring her team along, so she'd have her people around for support and confidence. But first, I wanted her to take some time off, just to be with me, so we could enjoy ourselves without stress. God, I couldn't wait to tell her my idea.

But I didn't get the chance because she ran out of my apartment before I could explain. I tried calling, but she wasn't picking up. I was worried, but I told myself if something had happened, I would know. Or at least I hoped so. I just needed to get to Icon Records, talk to her boss, and then scour the whole city until I found her.

It hurt to see her like that, so lost and desperate, but I promised I'd fix everything, and I meant it. If there was one thing I couldn't stand, it was letting my girl down. My new mission was to make Elena happy, no matter what. I wanted to see that gorgeous smile of hers every day, and if she needed to cry, I wanted it to be tears of joy. I could already picture us getting married, having kids. Just the thought of little Elenas running around made my heart race. It felt like a glimpse of heaven. I'd never even considered having kids before I met her, but now the idea of not having more of her in the world seemed unbearable. And I was more than ready to change that.

Alex sat next to me in the car, completely silent. He didn't know what was going on between us, so I used the ride to fill him in. To my surprise, he wasn't thrilled.

"I have no idea how I'm going to explain this to your sponsors," he muttered, lost in thought. "Let's hope they don't drop you."

"You're overreacting, dude." I took a deep breath. "I told you, everything will be fine."

"I don't understand how you can stay so calm. And I can't even imagine how Elena must be feeling right now. If you'd told me earlier, this album wouldn't have even come out. I would've pulled you out of here the moment I found out."

"And that's exactly why I didn't tell you." I shrugged. People needed to chill out.

The car stopped outside Icon Records, and we headed in. Jeremy was expecting us in his office, which pissed me off because I wanted to check if Elena was around. But there was no time. He stood by the door as we walked in, and I felt like a kid being scolded. Alex and I took seats across from Jeremy, who settled behind his desk, looking stern. For a moment, it felt like I was back in school, waiting for detention.

"Martin, I assume you're aware of what's happening. And I hope you understand the severity of your actions."

I didn't reply, just shifted uncomfortably in my chair.

"My question is simple, and once I have your answer and Elena's, the board will decide what to do with both of you."

"Jeremy, it's really not that serious, man," Alex tried to smooth things over. "They're young; it happens."

"Other clients were involved, Alex. It's not that simple."

"What's the question?" I interrupted, anxiety creeping in.

"Who initiated this? Who made the first move?"

This was it—time to put my plan into motion. I took a deep breath and closed my eyes.

"It wasn't me," I said confidently.

Jeremy's eyes widened, and Alex stared at me, stunned.

"Sam, this is a serious matter," Jeremy said, his voice tense. "Not only could Elena lose her job, she *will*. I'm going to ask you one last time: who started this?"

Like I cared. She'd be better off working for herself, in a fancy office with high-end clients. She'd earn double what she made at Icon and be happy forever.

"I told you, it wasn't me."

What was his problem? Was Jeremy getting old and losing his hearing? He started talking again, but I just wanted him to shut up. I still needed to find Elena and explain my plan, hoping she'd get on board. Oh, and I had to keep her away from that idiot John. He wasn't going to touch her again without going through me first. I could forgive Elena for cheating on me at that stupid party if she promised never to see him again. We definitely needed to talk about that.

Eventually, Jeremy let us go, saying he'd contact us once the board decided what to do. I rushed out of the building, ignoring Alex calling my name. I hailed a taxi and headed straight to Elena's place, cursing myself for not driving in the first place.

When the cab pulled up, I ran to her door, pounding on it like my life depended on it. Because, let's face it, it kind of did. I had to be the one to tell her what happened, not Jeremy or anyone else. If she misunderstood, I was dead.

I knocked again, but there was no answer. I tried peeking through the living room window, but the house was dark. She wasn't home. I ran a hand through my hair, starting to panic.

Elena had left my place on foot. I'd watched her from the balcony, walking south and turning the corner before I lost sight of her. Now I was picturing the worst—what if she was hurt, alone in some rundown hospital, when I could've been there, making sure she was in the best care in Toronto? Waiting at her house felt impossible. So I went back home, grabbed my car, and started scouring the city for her.

After two hours of aimlessly driving around Toronto, I called Elena for what felt like the millionth time. Okay, it was the twentieth, but still. My phone kept count, which was just rubbing it in. Since she didn't pick up, I sent another text:

Where are you? I've been driving around looking for you for hours! Please, answer the phone!

She got the message but didn't bother reading it. I threw my phone onto the passenger seat, feeling tears sting my eyes. Where the hell was she? Had she already been fired? God, I hoped not. If she was, I'd have to deal with her rage and try to fix things—if she'd even let me.

As the sun began to set, I felt completely lost. I had no idea where to go or what to think. All I could do was pray she was okay. I parked outside her house and sat there for hours, texting her over and over.

Please, Lena, answer the phone! I'm worried sick. Just tell me where you are and I'll come to you.

We need to talk. I can explain everything. I know you're upset, but it'll all be fine in the end, I promise!

It's almost ten p.m., and you're still not home. Where are you, Lena?

You said I could always wait for you. Please, come back. I love you!

I hesitated before hitting send. Confessing my love like this could either bring her to me or push her further away, but I couldn't keep it in. I loved her so much that being apart felt unbearable. I took a deep breath and grabbed the notebook and pen I kept in the glove compartment. Writing was my therapy, and I was desperate for it, or I'd lose my mind right there in the car.

"How many times will I have to die before you let us live?" I scribbled frantically, my hand shaking as I pressed the pen hard against the paper, leaving imprints on the pages beneath. "Let us be free. This should be the best moment of our lives.Meeting new people, new places and I'd get the chance to show you that you're the only one who matters."

I wasn't sure what I was doing, but once I started, I couldn't stop. Tears blurred my vision, some dripping onto the pages and smudging the ink. Where was she?

I must have dozed off in the car, lucky no one called the cops on me for sleeping there. Alex would lose it if I ended up on some gossip site for crashing in public like that. I woke up to sunlight streaming through the window. Her house looked just as quiet as it had last night. I couldn't tell if she'd come home or not. Maybe she'd snuck in after I passed out, and I hated myself for not staying awake. I should've watched the door all night.

I thought about knocking again, but if she was inside, I didn't want to wake her. Then again, what if she wasn't there? What if she'd left me? What if she was hurt somewhere, and I was just sitting here, doing nothing?

"Fuck!" I slammed my fist on the steering wheel and took a shaky breath. For the first time, my brain kicked in. I needed to go home, take a shower, eat something, and come up with a real plan to win her back.

The routine of "leaving my apartment, spending hours parked in front of Elena's house, then going back home" was now on its fifth day. I'd tried calling Icon Records, but no one would tell me a damn thing about her. The operator just repeated the same line about not giving out information on employees. At least that meant she was still part of the team. Maybe she was just taking some time off and would be back soon, which meant I still had a chance to find her. Not that I had any other choice: Elena was responsible—not just for every beat of my heart but also for the amazing marketing plan for my new album. Speaking of which, the release was only a few days away, and I couldn't wait for everyone to hear it. Even though my muse had freaked out over the lyrics, I was so proud to sing about her and our love that I could barely contain my excitement. A huge smile spread across my face as I remembered Elena calling them "shitty songs." I knew she didn't really mean it and would love them once she calmed down and actually listened to the words. They were my new treasure, and I'd sing them to her every morning until she begged me to stop. And then I'd write more songs about her and sing those too, until we grew old together.

Movement outside caught my attention, and I saw an older couple entering her house. They had a key, which struck me as odd. I'd seen photos of her parents before, so I knew they weren't hers. Her mom wasn't that old. I couldn't look away, and after what felt like forever, they came out. The man was on the phone, speaking excitedly to someone. That's when it hit me—Elena really wasn't home. Where the hell was she?

Without you, I'm nothing. An empty shell, soulless. You're the blessing I asked for, the light at the end of my journey. You're my person. Please, let us live.

A notification popped up saying the text couldn't be delivered, and I frowned. I tried calling her, but it went straight to voicemail. Maybe her phone had died, which was rare for Elena. She was always so prepared, carrying extra batteries everywhere.

About thirty minutes after the couple left, my world shattered—a guy in a suit put up a "sold" sign in front of her house. I stumbled out of the car, calling out to him.

"Hey." I tried not to sound desperate. "Do you know the owner of this house? She's a friend, and I've been trying to get in touch with her for days with no luck."

The man eyed me suspiciously, not a hint of recognition in his expression. "I don't, sorry," he said, sounding genuine. "I only dealt with someone named John, not a woman. Maybe you should ask him."

I stood there, alone on the sidewalk, as my world crumbled. Elena was with that asshole John. And if they were together, there was only one person who'd know where—Jeremy.

I drove to Icon Records like a maniac, fully expecting to get a stack of speeding tickets. That bastard was going to tell me where she was, or I wasn't Sam Martin!

"Whoa." Jeremy looked stunned when I burst into his office.

"Where is she?" I almost shouted. "Tell me, Jeremy. Where the hell is Elena?"

He stood up abruptly, fists clenched at his sides. "I have no idea where she is," he growled. "If you haven't noticed, she's not here anymore. Now get out, Martin. I've already lost my best marketing leader, and I swear there's nothing I'd like more than to punch you in the face. So get out!"

"Jeremy, please." I tried to rein in my desperation. "I need to talk to her. Please, help me. I'm begging you."

"Martin, I don't know where she is. The only thing I know is that Elena won't be coming back to this office, thanks to you!"

I ran my hands through my hair, tugging at it until it hurt. The operator had called her an employee; what did he mean, she wasn't coming back?

"Can you at least tell me if she's okay?"

Jeremy sighed and sank back into his chair. "No, Martin, I can't. I haven't spoken to her in days," he lied.

"She's with John, isn't she?" I asked, my voice dripping with bitterness.

"I'm not their babysitter; I have no idea."

He obviously knew but was shielding his friend from me. The man who loved Elena more than anything and just wanted to make things right with her.

"Sam." Jeremy sounded exhausted. "You've got a major release coming up. Go home, get some rest, and prepare yourself. You've got a busy year ahead, full of appearances and a tour—and it won't do you any good to chase her. Elena is moving on with her life, and there's nothing you can do about it. I'm sorry, but leave her alone. It's what's best for both of you."

Without another word, I left his office, glancing inside Elena's as I passed by. Her things were still there, and that gave me a shred of hope.

After Elena's house was sold, there was no point in sitting outside, waiting for her. The last time I drove by, I saw the curtains were gone, and the place was empty. My heart clenched, and I took a deep breath, trying not to cry.

It was the day of my concert, and I had rehearsal in a few hours. I'd prayed a million times, asking God to put a little voice in her head, telling her to come. I'm pretty sure even He was tired of me by now. Instead of going about my business, I parked outside Icon Records, hoping for just a glimpse of her, even if it was the last time. My plan was to convince her to come back to me so we could have a real conversation. By now, she probably knew what I'd said about us, and I wouldn't be surprised if she screamed at me on the sidewalk. But once she heard my reasons, she'd get it. She had to.

Then I saw them. Elena came out first, and I jumped out of the car, but then John appeared behind her, and I froze. They walked in the opposite direction, and my heart dropped when he pulled her close and wrapped his arm around her. I couldn't see her face clearly, but I saw him kiss the top of her head, and she wrapped her arm around his waist. They looked like one of those "relationship goals" couples you see online. He was perfect for her; they matched too well. His lion tattoo against her fair skin, his small eyes contrasting with her big, expressive ones, and their smiles... God, they looked so happy it made me sick.

That was the moment I realized I'd really lost her. And I couldn't even blame the guy. I was the one who messed up—me and my recklessness. As they walked away, reality smacked me in the face. I finally understood what she meant when she said I'd ruined everything. It was all my fault.

Not wanting them to see me, I ran back to my car and sped off to the stadium. Tears blurred my vision, and I had no idea how I'd get through the night. A part of me hoped she wouldn't show up, but deep down, I needed her there. I had to apologize for everything I'd done.

After the rehearsal, people started arriving. The whole Icon team was there, along with my family. My mom kept asking how I was doing. She knew about Elena and could tell I was a mess, but I couldn't help rolling my eyes when she asked, for the sixth time, if there was anything she could do. My parents were amazing, and my sister was my anchor, even when she wouldn't listen to my music.

"Is she here yet?" I asked Alex, and he shook his head.

"Sorry, Sam. We sent the VIP ticket to her office, but I don't know if she got it or if she's coming." I sighed and nodded. He gave me a supportive pat on the shoulder. "But it's showtime, so let's kill it, alright? The place is packed, and everyone's pumped to see you!"

He was right, of course. He got everyone out of the room, and I went through my warm-ups. Then I prayed for an incredible night and for the fans to have a great time—and I didn't forget to ask that they get home safely. Minutes later, we walked out, and the band took their spots on stage. The crowd went nuts, their screams so loud I could hear them through my earphones. I looked up and closed my eyes.

"This one's for you, Elena," I whispered and stepped on stage as the first chords of "You in Japan" started.

Seeing the packed venue made me smile. This was my place, where I belonged. I'd put my broken heart aside and give the fans everything I had. They were everything to me, and I couldn't let them down.

Performing those songs live for the first time was harder than I'd imagined. Each one held so many memories, and I found myself thinking about the moments when I wrote them. It was insane how people already knew the lyrics! The album had only dropped the day before, and it was already a hit—probably thanks to Elena's flawless marketing. I couldn't stop smiling and winking at the girls in the front rows. If they were here, it meant they'd arrived super early, and I wanted them to feel appreciated. My eyes scanned the crowd, silently acknowledging everyone. My mom was the best of them all, singing and dancing like she used to during school plays. It was super embarrassing back then, but right now, I wanted her on stage with me. And a few rows behind her, I saw Elena.

My heart flipped in my chest, and I grinned at her, but she didn't smile back. That was okay, though—she was here, and that was all that mattered. The night was perfect until I noticed that asshole John sitting beside her. My smile faded, and I turned back to the crowd.

"Thank you, everyone," I said when the song ended. "Before the next one, I want to give a shoutout to the incredible team at Icon Records who worked tirelessly to make this album and concert happen. Toronto, make some noise for them up there!"

I pointed to where they were seated, and the audience erupted. A roadie came up and took my guitar, as planned, and I walked to the piano. The next song wasn't on the setlist, but I had to play it. Elena needed to hear it, needed to know that I loved her and needed her. I took a deep breath and started playing.

"I didn't believe it, so I needed proof / Just one touch of your lips, and I knew it was true." I sang, my fingers moving over the keys. *"It was poison / And I drank the best of it all."*

This was tougher than I'd thought, and my eyes began to tear up. I wanted to get off the stage, apologize, and beg Elena for another chance, no matter who was watching.

"You sealed our fate / then set it ablaze." I looked up, and she was staring at me, shocked. *"But it was written in the stars / life was the death that tore us apart."*

I looked down at the piano, trying to focus. The audience was split between singing along and sitting in silence, and I even saw some girls crying. I smiled at them, feeling their pain—not for them, but for the girl who was here, tearing my heart apart like I was her personal puppet.

"We made a mess / But I can't stand to see you go." I looked at Elena again, willing her to remember our happiest moments. *"You're my whole world / So perfectly wrong for me."*

My heart stopped when she got up and left. John followed her, and in my wildest dreams, she'd have stormed the stage and hugged me, kissed me. But she didn't.

When the song ended, I felt hollow. Alex gave me a sympathetic smile from the wings, and I got up. I put myself on autopilot and finished the show, not really caring to switch off afterward.

EPILOGUE
Elena

JOHN AND I WERE WAITING AT THE DEPARTURE LOUNGE of Toronto Airport for our flight to New York. Boarding was in forty-five minutes, and I had to endure my friend's complaints the entire time. I was always extra cautious when flying, arriving at least two hours before boarding. Rebooking flights was a hassle and always meant losing money, and I couldn't afford that, not with a new life waiting for me in another country.

"You really need to stop whining," I told John as we wandered through a bookstore. "At least you won't miss the flight this time, unlike all those other times."

He rolled his eyes and followed me, reminding me of how much sleep he'd sacrificed because of my punctuality.

"I have no idea why I'm still friends with you. You're lucky I love you," he teased, making me stifle a laugh. "But you seem oddly cheerful today. What's up?"

I shrugged. "I cried my eyes out last night." I sighed, the weight of everything settling in. "But then I thought about it. If I'm starting fresh, I want it to be really new. I don't want to drag all that negative energy with me to New York. So I'm leaving it behind and deciding to give life another shot. I've done it before; why not do it again now?"

John hugged me and kissed the top of my head. "You're amazing, and I'm so proud of you." I looked up at him and grinned. "But we are never getting to an airport this early again!"

I made a face and stepped back. "Here's the deal: you stay here with your grumpy self while I run to the pharmacy."

Before he could protest, I walked out of the store. I had this thing for pharmacies—they had a way of making you buy things you didn't need and spend money you didn't have. Still, they were my favourite places to browse.

A few minutes later, I found myself chuckling at a display shelf. They'd lined up vibrators, condoms, and pregnancy tests in a neat little sequence. It seemed like a not-so-subtle warning: if you swap the vibrator for the real deal and skip the condoms, well, here's your next step.

But then something clicked, and guilt washed over me. I realized, almost panicking, that I should have had my period one, maybe two weeks ago. But there'd been nothing—no symptoms, no signs. My cycle was always clockwork, never a day late since I was twelve. I shook off the thought, certain it was just stress. But, before I knew it, I was grabbing a pregnancy test and heading to the self-checkout, shoving the box into my bag as I met John at the gate.

"I need to go to the bathroom," I whispered to John, hoping he'd let me through. We were in a row with only two seats, and he'd been kind enough to give me the window. I thought about waiting until we landed, but my anxiety was like a storm building inside me. I had to take the test now, or I'd lose my mind.

"You're kidding, right?" he muttered, irritated. "We've been in the air for like three minutes, and you went before we boarded."

I raised my brows. "Since when are you in charge of tracking my bathroom breaks? Come on, let me through!"

John sighed dramatically and got up. I practically ran to the bathroom, my purse clutched tight. My heart was pounding, and I thought I might faint. I stared at my reflection in the mirror, searching for any sign of change, any hint of what might be going on inside me. But I looked the same.

I read the instructions carefully and followed them to the letter. Peeing on a stick was harder than it sounded, especially with turbulence. I closed the blue cap and placed the test on the sink, as directed. I got dressed again and waited, trying to muster the courage to check the result. According to the box, one line meant I wasn't pregnant. Two lines meant…

"Fuck," I whispered when I lifted the test to eye level. Two bold lines stared back at me.

What now? I was on my way to another country, about to start a massive project with the company. I couldn't afford to go on maternity leave. Maternity—God, I wasn't ready for this.

I'd always wanted to be a mom. It was my biggest dream, but after years of marriage with no pregnancy, I figured it just wasn't in the cards for me. And now, here I was, in an airport bathroom, staring at a pregnancy test, panicking. I could barely manage my own life—how was I supposed to take care of someone else's? And what would my parents think? What would they say? Not to mention the baby's father, who was practically a kid himself. He was a reckless, spoiled teenager who had just thrown my life into chaos with a few love songs. I let out a bitter, involuntary laugh. He was actually the least of my worries, already a closed chapter in my book.

I leaned against the sink, closing my eyes as I muttered the only thing that came to mind:

"For fuck's sake, Martin!"

TO BE CONTINUED...

ACKNOWLEDGEMENTS

Perfectly Wrong came into being before I even realized it. A song or another on Spotify, a photo or video on Instagram, and the seed was planted. Shortly after, life took a sombre turn when my grandpa passed away. Suddenly, my ideas, my sadness and my yearning for a life that wasn't mine were all that remained.

Elena Vaughan and Sam Martin unwittingly became my cure. Countless days, afternoons, evenings, and nights were spent writing until my eyes burned, immersed in everything they wished to tell me. I cannot express how many sleepless nights I endured or how many lunch breaks at work I seized to sit at my desk and write feverishly, oblivious to the usual office noises around me. Elena and Sam were my world and the hands that held onto me during the two most overwhelming months of my life when I thought all I could do was fall apart. I could never adequately thank them for that.

However, they were not the only ones to help me lay the bricks in the construction of this story. I also had the unwavering support and dedication of a die-hard fan of theirs, who served as part of the inspiration behind Elena, with her mannerisms, emotional responses and all her wonderful retorts (for fuck's sake!). I'm lucky to be the godmother of her child and to call her my friend and business partner. Fernanda Segantini is truly an extraordinary person. Without her, Elena wouldn't be who she is, and Sam wouldn't even consider drinking Spanish wine. Thank you immensely, *amiga*!

Last but not least, I'm profoundly grateful for my grandfather Pedro, who imparted so much wisdom and with whom I shared countless incredible memories. He was the epitome of boundless strength. I will forever cherish and be immensely proud of him, but I will miss him even more. To borrow his words, **"Take a drink and fly, Elena!"**

ABOUT THE AUTHOR

MARIANA PEREIRA is a Brazilian writer whose literary journey is marked by passion, creativity, and determination. Her ability to create authentic and captivating characters draws readers in, while her range of themes and genres showcases her versatility as an author.

At 15, when she began exploring the world of fanfiction, Mariana demonstrated her talent for storytelling that captures readers' imaginations. Her first book, To My Idol, With Love, revealed her skill in writing romances with a touch of adventure, earning her a dedicated fan base. The book became a bestseller at three Bienal do Livro events. However, it was with Perfectly Wrong, the first Shawn Mendes fanfiction ever published worldwide, that Mariana took a significant step in her career. This book delves into profound themes, exploring issues like abusive relationships and social prejudices.

Inspired by renowned authors like Meg Cabot and Sophie Kinsella, Mariana strives to create strong and relatable characters that readers can connect with. Her love for reading and music, especially pop and pop rock, fuels her creativity and contributes to the development of immersive plots and atmospheres.

Mariana Pereira is more than a talented writer; she is an inspiring voice for other writers pursuing their dreams. Her message is clear: never stop honing your skills, seek guidance, and never give up on the gift of storytelling. With her talent and dedication, Mariana continues to enchant readers and pave her path to success in Brazilian literature.

Founded in 2024 as the international branch of Tulipa Editora, Tulipa Publishing was created to amplify the voices of Brazilian authors, offering a welcoming platform to bring their stories to readers worldwide. Though newly established, this publishing house brings the dedication and transformative vision of its parent company to the international stage.

Tulipa's mission is to provide an exceptional literary experience while offering authors a professional, fulfilling journey. Each project is handled with the utmost care, aiming to captivate readers and foster lasting partnerships. Their objective is to ensure every author feels inspired to return with new stories, confident in the supportive community that Tulipa provides.

The Tulipa Group has already brought a variety of works to life, including children's books and short story collections, enriching the Brazilian market with a unique voice. Now, as *Perfectly Wrong* debuts through Tulipa Publishing, this release is yet another step in Tulipa's growing legacy—a company that has already made its mark in Brazilian literature and is now extending its reach to readers everywhere.

www.ingramcontent.com/pod-product-compliance
Ingram Content Group UK Ltd.
Pitfield, Milton Keynes, MK11 3LW, UK
UKHW040604210726
13854UKWH00009B/2707